DEATH OUT OF NOWHERE!

Dan'l grinned and raised his left hand high to salute his companion's fast work. An eyeblink later, Dan'l roared like a wounded bear—a quartz-tipped lance had just punched into his upraised hand, ripping through the web of flesh at the base of his thumb.

Hellfire leaped down his arm. Dan'l reached up, snapped off the light reed lance, and drove the shaft clean through his hand. But when he looked up, his useless hand already swelling, the big explorer realized his troubles had just begun: A wild-eyed Comanche, face greased for battle, was closing in on him at a gallop, a bow in one hand, a fistful of arrows in the other!

DAN'L BOONE

MUSTANG DESERT

DODGE TYLER

LEISURE BOOKS NEW YORK CITY

Dedicated to a modern-day Dan'l,
Frank Joseph Soss, Jr.

A LEISURE BOOK®

April 1999

Published by

Dorchester Publishing Co., Inc.
276 Fifth Avenue
New York, NY 10001

ISBN 0-8439-4509-5

The name "Leisure Books" and the stylized "L" with design are trademarks of Dorchester Publishing Co., Inc.

Printed in the United States of America.

MUSTANG DESERT

Chapter One

"*There* is the man you must kill," announced Hugh Gilpin.

Gilpin, a former revenue collector for the Colony of Georgia, held out a portrait drawn in heavy black ink on a sheet of foolscap.

"Back east of the Great Muddy," he explained, "the Shawnee tribe call him Sheltowee—the name they reserve for their greatest enemy. He is Daniel Boone to the white men. But never mind white skin or red. In *any* man's language, his name spells misery for his enemies."

To impress his Indian audience, Gilpin spoke Spanish sprinkled with occasional words in Kiowa and Comanche. Two braves shared a small council fire with Gilpin, the tall Kiowa "contrary warrior" called River of Blood, and the Comanche

7

horse-riding champion known across the entire southwest frontier as Widow Maker.

River of Blood took the sketch from Gilpin and studied it for a long time. His young, handsome, sun-burnished face remained as inscrutable as granite. Then he handed it to Widow Maker.

His homely Comanche ally likewise studied it in attentive silence, taking the measure of Boone's square, weathered face and unruly hair, thick as a wild stallion's mane. Even this quick sketch had captured the clear and penetrating gaze.

"This is no ordinary whiteskin," Widow Maker finally announced. "He is *defiant*. See this hair on his face . . . only the free white men grow beards. Those who live in the whiteskin towns all scrape their faces clean. If not, their law-ways punish them."

"Never mind his hairy face," River of Blood scoffed. "Among eastern tribes, the Shawnees are no men to trifle with. Yet even they claim this Sheltowee is not mortal, that bullets aimed at him turn into sand."

Gilpin laughed, a harsh bark of contempt that echoed in fading ricochets across the early evening vastness surrounding them. The three men had met south of the Nueces River, in rolling land that rose into uneven hills sliced deep by arroyos. The Spanish, who claimed this territory as part of New Spain, called it the *grandes llamuras* or great prairies.

"Boone is a sly one," Gilpin said. "Also brave, cunning, and strong. And his trailcraft is matchless. But believe me, bullets can make him bleed."

"You have come many sleeps' ride," Widow Maker said. "Just to kill this one man? You say he is a threat to the entire red nation, dangerous as a smallpox blanket. But how?"

"To you red men," Gilpin said, "all of this"—one arm swept out, indicating the vastness—"is simply the Great Stealing Road into Sonora. You use it to raid the Mexicans. But to the Spaniards, this land is the Mustang Desert. This vast range, between the drainages of the Nueces River and the Rio Grande, is home to all their immense herds of wild horses. Thus, it is the key to their New World treasure."

It was River of Blood's turn to show contempt. He pointed toward a little fourteen-hand buckskin tethered nearby, taking off the grass. Human hands painted in red on the horse's hips symbolized scalps the Kiowa had taken.

"Do you mistake us for whelps sucking at the dug?" the Kiowa demanded of Gilpin. "Count our scalps. Look how heavy our coup sticks are. Why do you think we Kiowas and Comanches have tolerated these Christian *Gachupines* in our ancestral ranges for so long? Because they have raised our fine horses for us, *that* is why! If we tolerate so many of them, why not one Daniel Boone also?"

Gilpin nodded, showing no weakness. The British loyalist knew Indians well. So before he came west he had replaced his breeches and stockings with crude animal skins and knee-length moccasins. But he had also wisely retained his powdered wig and cocked tricorn hat—most Indians found them impressive, associating them with a shaman's regalia.

"The *Gachupines*," Gilpin retorted, using the local Indian term of contempt for the Spaniards, "are not your chief enemy. They mainly want to keep intruders out of Mexico and the silver mines there. Boone and his rabble are your worst enemy. He is one of these new rebels who call themselves *Americans*. They mean to steal all your horses and sell them in the white settlements. That's why Boone is out here now. And next it will be your hunting ranges they take. Then your women, and finally your very manhood."

This time there was no glint of contempt in either brave's lidded, evasive eyes. For it did indeed appear that this arrogant Sheltowee was tracking wild horse herds in the Mustang Desert.

"You Indians," Gilpin continued mercilessly, "will be kept off horses by law. You will be prevented from owning weapons or hunting buffalo. You will be turned into praying Indians and dirt-scatterers who answer roll calls—flea-ridden beggars like the Hopis and Papagos. Boone means to make squaws out of you."

Gilpin had recently given up his job as revenue collector to become a private "Indian agent" out west for his employer, Georgia Colony Governor Sir Lansford Stratton. Gilpin's job was to further Stratton's latest profit venture—to "clear the path of all that cumbers it," in Stratton's phrase. And the biggest obstacle right now was Daniel Boone.

Gilpin's words just now were carefully chosen

to chafe these proud warriors like burrs under a saddle blanket. And he succeeded.

"Boone will die a hard death," River of Blood vowed. "This place hears me when I swear he *will* go under! I am a Kaitsenko. You know what that means?"

Gilpin nodded, satisfied. Outwardly calm, he was joyous within. For that vow meant special trouble for Boone. Among the Kiowa tribe, the Kaitsenko Society represented the elite top ten percent of the warriors—only the hardest of the blooded fighters. Once a Kaitsenko swore publicly to kill an enemy, as River of Blood had just done, there could be only one of two outcomes: Either the enemy died, or the Kaitsenko fell on his own knife as the price for failing to kill.

"We will kill him," Widow Maker chimed in. "His teeth will rattle in a gourd at the scalp dance! His gut will lace our new moccasins! But we are not killing him so *you* may sleep easy, white eyes!"

"Como no," Gilpin replied. "Of course not. We are all mature men, we know how the world works. An empty hand is no lure for a hawk! I told you in great detail already what my Eagle Chief back east will pay you for this kill. Two large wagonloads of first-rate trade goods. Everything from muskets to calico and sugar."

"And strong water?" River of Blood demanded.

"Whiskey too, yes. You two will be the richest *indios* from here to where the sun goes down. Once you give me proof of the kill, I am authorized to set the wagons rolling out of the trading post at Nacogdoches."

"I have ears for this," Widow Maker said. "But once we kill Boone, you, Hugh Gilpin, will roll nowhere until those goods are delivered. *Entiendes?* You understand?"

Gilpin nodded. "Don't worry. You kill Daniel Boone, and those goods are just the beginning. My Eagle Chief has further plans that require good men like you. But we must trot before we canter. First kill Boone."

One day's fast ride west of this meeting place, the rolling hills gave way to steep mesas and broad grasslands dotted with juniper and sage. Big alkali sinks offered brackish but usually drinkable water. In places scoured by fierce, unbroken winds, the ground turned to desert hardpan.

Across a stretch of this pan, the clip-clop of shod hooves made cracking noises like bones snapping. Two riders, both big men and heavily armed, were following a few hundred yards behind a sizable *manada*—the Southwest word for the normal mustang unit, a master stallion and his band. Now and then, clumps of purple sage crackled underfoot, releasing its distinctive odor. Dust rose in crazy swirls around both riders, then settled, to powder the scant brush.

One of the men wore a ratty flap hat and rode a big mule with a sheepskin pad for a saddle; the other wore a broad plainsman's hat and rode an ugly coyote dun with a line down its back. The fenders of his Mexican vaquero saddle were trimmed in silver conchos.

"They're heading to water now," Dan'l Boone

announced with weary satisfaction, watching the band from the saddle of his lineback dun. "See Poco Loco watching them birds circle yonder? He done that at sunup, too. He knows birds fly to water at dawn and sunset."

Poco Loco was Dan'l's name for the "little bit crazy" lead stallion, who prided it over nearly a dozen mares in this band. Dan'l's companion halted his mule with a quick squeeze of his knees.

"That rings right," agreed Snowshoe Hendee. "Wunst 'em critters tank up good, they'll be loggy and slow. Give us a breather, Dan'l boy."

Dan'l nodded, watching the wild horses leaping and curvetting: the stallions, the brood mares, the suckling colts, the fillies. About a hundred fine animals in this *manada*. For weeks now Dan'l and Snowshoe had patiently trailed them across the Wild Horse Desert, living on buffalo hump and tainted water, tying themselves in the saddle to sleep. But with infinite patience, they had finally learned the band's range and habits.

"Them's some mean, broom-tailed broncos," Snowshoe opined. Like Dan'l, he was bearded. But Snowshoe tied his red beard in long, twin braids that he combed out twice daily.

It was Dan'l who'd come up with the nickname Snowshoe for Jeddiah Hendee. Both men had been trapped in an ice storm up in the Ohio Valley, Dan'l badly wounded after a skirmish with Miamis. Jeddiah fashioned crude snowshoes out of hides wrapped around bent willow frames. Then he carried his unconscious friend more than

13

two miles, through a raging blizzard, to a safe camp.

But Snowshoe paid for his heroism when frostbite forced the amputation of his left foot. Now he got along with a wooden foot he had carved himself from the sturdy osage tree. An ingenious system of buckles and straps held it in place. He limped like a peg-leg sailor. But Dan'l knew damn well that wooden foot was no liability when his friend was on horseback—Snowshoe could hang on like a tick and ride until he had the meanest bronco lipping salt out of his hand.

"And say!" Snowshoe added. "Would you jist *look* at all 'em colors and markings! Why, shoo! Bays, blacks, calicos, gingers, grays, claybanks—reg'lar mongrels. Ain't no horses look like that back in the settlements."

"No," Dan'l agreed. "All you'll see back there are blacks and whites and big chestnut bays. But a good horse can never be of bad color. And these're good horses, I'll warrant. The best."

"Ahuh," Snowshoe grunted. "Tough as any grizz and all bottom. Mister, they've wore this child down to the hubs. But I ain't so sure they'll sell. 'Sides being queer-looking, them's *puny* animals, Dan'l. Hosses back east run seventeen hands, these here is maybe fourteen at best. Little squirts."

"'Praise the tall, but saddle the small,'" Dan'l retorted, quoting a Spanish saying. "The word you want is small, not puny. Once folks study on these animals a mite, they'll see which way the wind sets. These little mustangs is the future of this west country, happens it's gonna have one."

Dan'l and Snowshoe had spent the cool snow-melt months trapping and hunting their way into the heart of the little-explored Wild Horse or Mustang Desert. Now, to profit off their long return trip, they meant to trail, trap, and break to leather a herd of wild Spanish stock.

Eventually, they meant to drive them back to the Colonies for breed stock. These exotic, hearty Southwest breeds were much talked about—but also much maligned as inferior "Indian scrubs." Dan'l was convinced the public would pay top dollar for them once the mustang's many virtues were fully understood. It was not the color that made a horse, as the Spanish knew. It was the *brío escondido*, the "hidden vigor" that gave value to a horse.

From studying them over time, Dan'l now realized what most men back east had yet to grasp: Horses were not just dray animals, fit to plow furrows, uproot stumps, tow barges, and pull conveyances. Because of the vast distances out here, horses would in fact be the key to all frontier enterprise. Out here, even land meant less than horses.

Dan'l's thoughts scattered when he noticed Poco Loco slowing the band. He was interrupting their journey to water so they could graze a good patch of grass.

As usual, the leader sent a "spy" stallion back to study these odd men. Dan'l had noticed how social these wild horses were. They often rushed up to inspect the men's camp. Dan'l had seen horses, separated from their *manada*, take up with a herd of buffalo.

This old spy stallion had lost a chunk of his nose in a past battle with wolves or panthers. While he kept an eye on the men from a close distance, Poco Loco, too, was vigilant. Dan'l watched him stretch his head as high as he could, looking and smelling constantly between mouthfuls of grass.

Snowshoe, watching Dan'l and the master stallion lock stares, loosed a rattling chuckle. "That bronc's a tough'n, Dan'l. But I do believe he's met his match in Squire Boone's ugliest son, Dan'l. Not only are you good at horseback thinking—you're tricky as a red-headed woman!"

Snowshoe swung down off his mule and tilted back a bladder bag of mescal, swallowing a few jolts. Then he poured some into his hat and offered it to the mule, who slurped it greedily.

Dan'l's strong white teeth flashed through his beard. "You get that cantankerous animule drunk, Snowshoe, we'll both regret it."

"Boone, do I look like I just fell off the turnip wagon? Don't you fret none. Malachi holds his coffin varnish better'n most men can."

The blood-red ball of sun dipped even lower. Poco Loco bunched his group again and resumed the run north to water.

"Think we can pen 'em soon?" Snowshoe called over to Dan'l. Each man led a packhorse by a lead-line tied to his bridle.

Dan'l nodded. "Now we know all their water holes, we can block 'em off. Force the bunch to one water spot *we* pick. We do a good job disguising the holding pen, we can have 'em trapped in three days."

"By God, this child hopes so, Dan'l." Snowshoe glanced all around them in the gathering darkness. "By now somebody knows we're out here running horses. The Espanish figger them herds is theirs. So do the local tribes. Might be lead flying around here right damn quick."

"Then let it fly!" Dan'l retorted in a hearty tone, tossing back his head and laughing at all Creation. "You know Boone's Rule: Only take bachelors. Stinking old toothless one-footed goat like you, hell. Where's the loss if you get kilt?"

Dan'l was only roweling, but Snowshoe was cranky from exhaustion. He scowled so deeply that his shaggy red eyebrows touched. But before he could fire a return volley, Dan'l's excited voice cut him short.

"Well, I'm a Dutchman! Look yonder, Snowshoe! Up on that ridge! See him?"

Snowshoe slewed around and followed the end of Dan'l's finger.

"Why, God's trousers!" the big trapper exclaimed. "It's ... Katy Christ, Dan'l! It's the Pacer!"

Up on the distant ridge, magnificent in the glorious blaze of dying sunlight, glided a beautiful white stallion. And *glide* was precisely what it seemed to be doing, Dan'l marveled. He moved like a white shadow, hardly seeming to work his legs. When he paused, his magnificent tail touched the ground; in motion, he constantly tossed his head to keep the mane from his eyes.

Both riders drew rein, staring in thrilled disbelief. For both of them knew the Southwest legend about the famous "Pacing White Mustang." Incapable of running or trotting, the white pacer could nonetheless never be captured, according to lore, unless it allowed itself to be—which it sometimes did.

The Pacer symbolized freedom for all wild horses. Its sole purpose was evidently to "steal" horses away from men, to lead domesticated animals back to freedom. Indian legend said that any red man who mounted the Pacing White Mustang could ride him to *la cola del mundo*, "the tail end of the world."

"By God, he's at easy creasing distance!" Snowshoe exclaimed. "He's ours now!"

A British-made Ferguson musket protruded from a long boot on Snowshoe's sheepskin pad. He reached for it, his eyes aglint as he calculated distance and windage and elevation. Snowshoe was expert at the controversial art of "creasing"— temporarily stunning a wild horse by grazing its spine with a bullet.

But Dan'l stayed his friend's hand with a grip like an eagle's talons. Dan'l didn't approve of creasing. If a man aimed wrong by less than one inch, the horse was dead or ruined for life. It was quick and easy when it worked, cruel and deadly when it didn't. Dan'l had never favored the lazy way around a hard job.

"What in Sam Hill is wrong with you, Boone?" Snowshoe exploded even as the Pacer glided out of sight again. "The sumbitch is gone now, you goldang fool!"

"Never mind gone," Dan'l said quietly, taking a careful glance all around them in the grainy twilight. "Happens that really was the Pacer, you best worry about the fact that we even saw him in the first place. You take my meaning?"

For a moment Snowshoe continued cursing, paying no attention to Dan'l's pensive words and tone. Then, all of a moment, Snowshoe remembered the rest of the legend about the Pacing White Mustang. His face turned white as new linen above his beard. Like Dan'l, he was highly respectful of folk tales.

It was rare, said the legend, for any white men to actually spot the Pacing White Mustang. In fact, such rare sightings were always an omen, a grave warning. A dire warning. Any whiteskins who spotted the Pacer, Dan'l and Snowshoe both recalled, soon had an appointment with death.

Chapter Two

"Gentlemen! Even now, as we meet, my capable Indian agent is on a peaceful mission in the Far West. I have sent Hugh Gilpin to study these 'Indian scrubs' first-hand. To observe the red aborigines as they employ these mixed-breed horses in their crude, nomadic lifestyles. Hugh is on a fact-finding mission only. But I am convinced that his report will only bolster what we already know about these vastly inferior scrub ponies."

Sir Lansford Stratton, Colonial Governor of Georgia, paused to tamp a bit of snuff behind his upper lip. Then he tucked the silver snuffbox back into the ruffled sleeve of his velvet doublet. He resumed his dramatic pacing at the head of a raw plank lecture hall packed with men and spittoons.

"Gentlemen! Only consider this Spanish word,

bronco! It translates 'rough.' Now, an apt synonym for a 'rough' horse is an 'unfinished' horse. A crude horse. A common, inferior horse. These *broncos*—their bloodlines are hopelessly mongrelized! If we tolerate the introduction of these animals to our colonies, they will permanently dilute the purity of our American quarter horses."

"Hear, hear!" someone shouted.

"Solid colors, especially bay or chestnut, are the natural and perfect trait of a well-bred horse. Big-boned, deep-chested animals directly descended from Arabian steeds and the so-called Barbs of the Barbary States."

"The Gov'nor has struck a lode there!" another enthusiast exclaimed. "He's your boy when the topic turns to horses!"

Stratton smiled modestly at the compliment. The Governor had recently penned a widely popular pamphlet titled *Equitation in the American Colonies.* It was already considered the authority on horses and horse breeding in the New World—an engrossing topic to most colonists.

This lecture in the interior settlement of Albany, Georgia, was part of Stratton's campaign to establish his "Continental Standard" for horses—unrivaled use of the very animals he had just described as ideal. Carefully sniffing the winds of fortune, Stratton had invested most of his wealth in the breeding of such horses. Now it was essential to ensure a brisk demand for them.

"These *broncos* . . . their ugly, erratic markings, their bizarre range of colors, prove the fault of discipline in their breeding. Thus they are the 'runts' of the equestrian litter. Small, weak, less intelligent, less durable. Of *course* men like Daniel Boone enthusiastically champion these *broncos*. After all, Boone is a human *bronco*! His blood, too, is hopelessly mixed and watered down to common stock."

This time Stratton's scorn drew fewer cheers. Although none in this mostly Tory crowd dared say it, Daniel Boone's name was beginning to stand for a bold new defiance—a desire for freedom that was about to flare up like a conflagration, fanned by the winds of Old World oppression and taxation.

"Boone has openly boasted," Stratton resumed, "that he means to drive a herd of these *mestizo* horses east. But the Yellow River will run clear first! Military cartographers and scouts insist there is *no* possible route across the Great Desert of the West—not for a herd of stock dependent on ample water and grain.

"An ancient proverb says, 'For every noble horse that neighs, a hundred asses set up their discords.' Discordant asses like Daniel Boone! Vulgar mountain rabble who are urging us to place our fortunes on the swayed backs of mongrel horses!"

Again lusty cheers greeted Stratton's remarks. One man seated on the front bench, however, seemed bored by the proceedings.

He was a big, swarthy man with eyes gray as morning frost and a chiseled face. He wore butternut homespun and an impressive brace of pistols, all cocked and primed. An old dueling scar marred his right cheek.

The only time he showed any reaction at all was when Stratton mentioned Daniel Boone. Then the man smiled briefly with his lips only, the eyes cold and dead as bone buttons.

The Cherokee princess, called Sarah Ferguson by her father's people, lived in the Cherokee Overhill town of Chota. But several times each year, she traveled east to the whiteskin town of Albany.

The Indian princess made this long journey solely to study the newest "fashion babies" on display in dressmakers' shops. These twenty-four-inch mannequins were sent over directly from Europe, dressed in the latest fashions and complete in all accessories. Thus, women on the very fringes of civilization could stay abreast of clothing fashions.

Sarah was known as Sha-hee-ka, or "Beautiful Death Bringer," to her red mother's people. Her title of princess came by right of birth. However, by right of proven combat, she was also a member of the highly respected Cherokee Ghighau or Beloved Women.

Known also as the War Women, the Ghighau were present by law at every war council. Among Cherokees, all women had special status. But chivalry had nothing to do with it. It was because women were the mothers of warriors, and thus deserved honor. And of course, women who had themselves won honors in war were doubly worthy of respect.

Now, as Sha-hee-ka stood in Albany's Warickshire Lane studying a fashion baby in a shop win-

Dodge Tyler

dow, she drew many curious and admiring
glances herself. She had combed her long black
hair smooth and close, then plaited it. Her eyes
were big and almond-shaped, her lips full, her
nose long and aristocratic, reflecting the blood of
her father. She wore a dyed buckskin skirt and a
short jacket secured with silver broaches, reveal-
ing a few inches of bare, taut midriff.

Sha-hee-ka concentrated, memorizing the pat-
tern of a handsome rick-rack braiding on a gown.
Abruptly, a motion in the corner of her eye made
her glance across the rutted street.

Two men, absorbed in conversation, were just
then entering the Turk's Head Inn. The moment
Sha-hee-ka recognized them, her skin tingled with
cool apprehension.

The plump, self-satisfied man in the powdered
wig and fustian breeches was Lansford Stratton,
a two-faced liar who offered the red man one hand
in friendship while the other hid a knife behind
his back.

The other man—stone-faced, stone-eyed, light
on his feet like a stalking cat—was a Russian. A
former free trapper named Lev Vogel. Russians
had once established a few trading posts in America, only to be driven out early on. Vogel, however,
had remained behind to head a "private army" of
former trappers who'd been squeezed out.

Sha-hee-ka knew that Vogel's bunch were an
"army" in name only. They were murderers—
thieving cutthroats for hire. "Free lances" as mercenaries were termed in her father's country. And
if Vogel was meeting with Lansford Stratton, it

could only mean that serious treachery was afoot. Sha-hee-ka had been caught up once before in the web of Stratton's greedy ambitions.

She knew the territory where Vogel's ragtag militia camped: a series of pine bluffs near the headwaters of the Savannah River. Now, watching these two evil, corrupt men slip into the Turk's Head, Sha-hee-ka made a resolution: She would journey even farther and keep a close eye on Vogel's camp.

She had to. With some sixty-four Cherokee towns scattered around in this region, Stratton's latest treachery might well involve her people. Sha-hee-ka resolved to find out whatever she could.

"They say Boone is marked out from other men," Stratton told Vogel. "There are men whom bees will not sting. And Boone, according to Dame Rumor, is one of them."

"That's claptrap," Vogel replied quietly in heavily accented English. "I can respect a man's cunning without turning him into a God. Boone is no man's fool. If I was rich like you are, I would stay clear of him. But I am getting light in the pocket and need paying work."

"Of course it will pay. I didn't ask you to come all this way so that we could quibble over a few shillings. Just remember, you and your men may never actually be needed. This is just an assurance."

"We burn powder only if he makes it to the Mississippi with horses, right?"

Stratton nodded, sipping from a pony glass of brandy. The two men shared a deal table at the rear of the Turk's Head. "Only if he makes it to the river with horses, correct. And if fortune is a good wench, Lev, he never will. Boone will rot in a nameless grave out in the Great Desert."

Stratton fell silent, brooding for some time with his face set in a tight frown like a carved mask. Once before, Daniel Boone's interference had ruined his plans and nearly cost him his fortune. Now Stratton was determined to kill Boone. Or at least ruin his fortunes. If that bearded upstart were allowed to arrive with wild horses, it would set a dangerous precedent.

King George and his loyalists had kept most of the settlers in their place by insisting that the Great American Desert beyond the Mississippi River was mostly useless—that it offered no profit whatsoever to those back east in the Land of Steady Habits.

Boone's success, should that be permitted, would encourage the homespun rabble to greater insubordination. Even worse, it might jeopardize Stratton's control of the market for horses and horse breeds.

"I'll move my men west and set up a camp," Vogel said. "If he makes it to the river with horses, he'll have to ford at Dick's Ferry near Frenchman's Lick. But why are you so sure Boone won't make it back to civilization?"

Stratton's lips formed a grim, wire-tight smile. "Because a man may meet with many terrible disasters on the wild frontier. Natural or . . . man-made."

Vogel snorted. "Yes, but *this* man's clover grows deep. Boone has survived plenty of disasters."

"Yes he has," Stratton agreed. "Many of them. But that's precisely my point. You see, the bucket can be carried once too often to the well. Boone's luck is finally due to run out."

Chapter Three

"That'll do 'er, hoss," Dan'l called out to Snowshoe. "Be at least a few days before they water here again. Should give us enough time, happens we can work quick enough."

Dan'l had just used a bone awl to poke a hole in all four corners of an old saddle blanket. Now, using rawhide tie-downs, he and Snowshoe had secured the blanket in a patch of the stubby growth called *palo duro*. It grew right next to a clutch of rocks surrounding a frothing spring. This was one of the favorite watering holes of the band commanded by the roan stallion Dan'l called Poco Loco. But the presence of any new object bearing the man smell would spook mustangs.

"That only leaves the one hole that we ain't

marked," Dan'l added. "And that's where we pen the bunch."

"We by-god better pen 'em, and right damn quick," Snowshoe grumbled. "We're out of meal and salt and eating tobaccy. And there's been one night too many, Sheltowee, spent sleeping in a goldang Santa Fe bed."

Dan'l grinned, the corners of his eyes crinkling like old shoe leather. A "Santa Fe bed," as every yondering pioneer knew, was made by lying on your stomach and covering that with your back. But their plight wasn't just comical. Squire Boone had taught all his boys to thank God for a healthy stomach, and Dan'l knew from grim experience why that was crucial to an explorer.

Delicate digestion would sink a man out here. For long weeks now it had been nothing but hastily charred buffalo or antelope meat and tepid, brackish water. No bread, no fruit, and no vegetables except a few wild onions. Becky, Dan'l mused with a longing belly, never served a meal without greens and a fresh-fruit cobbler. And he'd give a purty for one of her pan biscuits soaked in pot liquor.

But it wasn't just the piddlin' victuals. Trailing a band of wild mustangs across their vast ranges was some of the hardest work Dan'l had ever tackled. That range included crossing the fiercest desert in northern Mexico, the Bolsón de Mapimí.

At night, when clouds obscured the polestar, the men lost all bearings in this strange new country. Then they were forced to use the wind as their compass, for in the Mustang Desert country it nearly always blew from the southwest.

And then, thought Dan'l as he lifted a stirrup out of his way to tighten the dun's girth, there were signs of new trouble forming like a bad storm. Other signs besides seeing the omen of the Pacing White Mustang.

Snowshoe, reading Dan'l's careworn face, spoke up abruptly.

"Talk out, Sheltowee! You're thinkin' *we're* being trailed ourselfs, just like we're trailin' that band—ain'tcher? You seen them dust puffs earlier today."

"Ain't just dust puff, hoss."

Dan'l crossed to a nearby pile of crusted horse droppings. He broke some open with the toe of his boot.

"The mustangs we're trailing graze mostly palomilla grass and sotol stalks. Our animals eat palomilla and the little grain we give 'em. But *these* horses have grazed bunchgrass near a big river. The droppings're different—dryer and lighter, see it?"

Snowshoe scowled, tugging at the twin red braids of his beard. "You're sayin' there's horses on this range besides mustangs and our own?"

"That's the way of it, hoss. Injun ponies—they ain't shod."

Both men mulled this as they finished checking their cinches and latigos, preparing to move out again. So far, during long weeks in this lonesome country, they had encountered almost no one, just a few peaceful Indians, and once, a group of elegantly dressed Mexican gentlemen-horsemen, or *charros*, on their way to Santa Fe to pay their land taxes.

"Even though it's red men on our trail," Dan'l added, "mayhap it's white men what put 'em there."

Snowshoe squinted. "Stratton's work?"

"Or the devil's. It's all one. Stratton knows we're out here by now. Word has it he's let Hugh Gilpin off his leash—got him out here stirring up the tribes."

"Aye, that's Stratton." Snowshoe spat into the dust. "He's alla time harping on that damned Proclamation Act. Says can't nobody go west of a line drawed by King George. Why, swamp fog! Old Stratton's got *his* toad-eaters out here staking out tomahawk claims. And he means to free you from your soul, Boone! Stratton won't *never* forget how you put the hobbles on him out in the Arkansas country. You damn near ruinated him that time, Dan'l."

Dan'l grinned as he swung up into leather. "No, ol' Stratton can't abide this child, can he? Stratton likes to keep everybody on a short leash. But us Boones always was hard dogs to keep under the porch."

For a moment, before they rode out to find the mustangs again, Dan'l took a long, searching look all around them. He was seeing what few white men had yet seen: the West, where a man could look farther, yet see less of anything but land and sky.

Out here, Dan'l mused, a man had plenty of

wheeling distance, all right. But those same wide-open spaces were beyond all law—one giant, un-marked grave just waiting to be filled.

"Boone and the red-beard have made camp for the night," River of Blood announced upon returning from a brief scouting mission. "And brother, for-tune rides with us. Truly they have camped in their own graves!"

The tall Kiowa sprang from the back of his little buckskin and quickly ground-tied it with a buffalo-hair rope. Widow Maker, busy stringing a new bow, put his work aside. The two renegades had made a cold camp in the lee of a redrock butte. Moonlit expanses of juniper and sage stretched out toward the horizons.

"If you have some news," the Comanche said, impatience edging into his voice, "speak it or bury it! Are we young girls playing guess-my-dream?"

River of Blood felt too exultant to show anger at this scorn. He slid a flint-tipped arrow from his quiver and used it to draw in the dirt. As he knelt, his bone breast-plate rattled.

"They have blocked all the band's water holes except this one," River of Blood said, poking a hole in the dirt, "at Buffalo Creek. Now they are camped in the flat-grass slope above the creek. In the *middle* of it," he added triumphantly. "Buck, do you know how tall and dry that grass is by now?"

Even Widow Maker, who seldom found reason to rejoice in anything, could not resist a satisfied grin.

"Of course," he replied. "The same way we routed the Lippan Apaches at the Brazos River. We will make a wheel of fire and trap them in it while they sleep."

River of Blood nodded, making a big circle in the dirt with the arrow point. "We wait until Uncle Moon reaches his zenith. By then they will be asleep and the hard night winds from Old Mexico will be stirring. While we wait, we make fire bundles from dry sotol stalks and plant them in a circle. Then, you start here, I here, and we ride quickly around, igniting the bundles with torches. I am a good rider, brother, and you are the best. We can have an unbroken wheel of fire before those two wake."

Widow Maker grunted agreement. "This plan has merits. That grass is so high now it brushes a pony's belly. And so dry that it rustles like old wasp nests in a light breeze. With the night winds howling, it will burn faster than even an antelope could outrun it. Before Sister Sun wakes up tomorrow, the mighty Sheltowee will be maggot fodder!"

"Now damnit, Malachi!" Snowshoe cursed his mule. "You slip that tether agin, old campaigner, and I swan I'll hobble you!"

Dan'l laughed as he watched his companion limp back into the circle of firelight, leading his rebellious mule. The problem was that the mustangs were now bedded down close by, and Malachi was love-struck. All mules were devoted to mares, and Malachi "had a case," as Dan'l put it, on one of the master stallion's favorite mares, a little *grullo* or blue with white stockings. All night the pining mule had tried to join the mustangs to be near its beloved.

Despite his laughter, however, Dan'l continued his careful cleaning and inspection of all his weapons, laid out on a waterproof groundsheet in the flickering firelight: his breech-loading flintlock musket, its breech plug modified so that Dan'l could remove it without a wrench, and thus get off four shots per minute; a .38 caliber flint pistol with over-and-under barrels, in a well-oiled holster on a heavy gunbelt; and the curved skinning knife that was always tucked into boot or moccasin.

"Start the catch pen tomorrow?" Snowshoe demanded, busy using a hog-bristle brush to comb ticks and debris out of his beard.

Dan'l nodded. "We'll have to haul in brush to disguise the wings. And then hire on some local Indians as bronco busters. I ain't got the tailbone to break a hunnert horses."

"Aww, break a cat's tail, Boone! That white pacer we seen was only one hoss. Coulda broke him in two days. You tarnal fool, Dan'l, how's come you stayed my hand? Why, that animal would fetch us two bits a peek, was we to put it on display back in the settlements."

"You don't want to capture a horse that prideful," Dan'l rebuked him. Dan'l had known of especially proud stallions, once they were penned, to die of what the Spaniards called *despecho*—indignation, wrath, nervous excess.

The wind whipped up, stirring the long grass all around them and making the campfire flames saw crazily. That wind also brought a foul-smelling whiff to Dan'l's nostrils. It was Snowshoe's infamous body odor, subject of much trail lore.

Dan'l shifted around the fire until he was upwind of his friend.

"Snowshoe," he said fondly, "you're steady as bedrock, and I owe you my life. But, hoss, it's God's truth: The stink blowing off you is strong enough to drop a buffalo in its tracks."

"Tell you what, Boone," Snowshoe shot back. "You show me the best-smelling man with the fanciest feathers and the biggest rowels on his spurs. And *that's* the boy you best avoid like a bad habit. Sweat and glamour don't mix, Sheltowee."

"Mebbe so, but sweat 'n' soap does."

"Ahh, kiss my lily-white, you little barber's clerk."

It was a familiar old argument with them, fought without rancor. In reality, both men were busy monitoring the darkness out beyond the circle of firelight. Dan'l had carefully avoided gazing directly into the flames so he would not ruin his night vision. Because both men felt it: the presence of someone watching them.

Dan'l filled his powder flask and cleaned the sand from his shot pouch. Then he laid his weapons out so they'd be close to hand.

"Take turn-about on guard duty?" Snowshoe suggested reluctantly.

Dan'l considered. They were both dog-tired. And they had a few days of back-breaking labor ahead of them to capture that *manada*. Neither man had slept well in weeks. Dan'l debated: His lineback dun had been trained to hate the Indian smell, and so had Malachi. It should be safe in this wide-open space.

"No guard tonight," he finally replied. "We ain't 'zacly safe as sassafras here, but it's a fair-to-middlin' position to defend. Get you some sleep, hoss. You'll need it."

Out beyond the circle of light, a lone coyote raised its mournful, ululating howl. The sound trailed off in a series of yipping barks.

Dan'l rolled into his buffalo robe and thought again about seeing the white pacer earlier. He pulled his long gun closer even as the wind rose to a mournful shriek like lost souls in torment.

In his troubling dream, Dan'l smelled the acrid stink of hot smoke, felt the stinging pinpricks of tiny sparks on his face.

He was chasing the mysterious Pacing White Mustang along a steep ridge. Suddenly, they reached a blind cliff. The pacer leaped out over the dark chasm, and before Dan'l could rein in, his lineback dun leaped out behind the mustang.

Only as he began to plummet to his death did Dan'l look down and see that the chasm below him was brilliantly aflame—beckoning to him like the maw of Hell itself!

Then, somewhere in the real darkness nearby, a horse snorted the signal for flight. That noise made Dan'l abruptly sit up, one hand seizing his pistol.

"Well, I'm a Dutchman! Snowshoe! Up and on the line, hoss. *Now!*"

The entire prairie around them was on fire. A burning ring of flames was about to close in on them. Dan'l watched Poco Loco furiously driving his near-panicked band through the last small opening. The master stallion bit laggards, rammed them along with his head. He even killed a young colt, quickly snapping its neck in a powerful bite, so a mare would quit hanging back.

Dan'l gave thanks to God Almighty when the last of the mustangs made it to safety, though he groaned aloud as they scattered to hell and gone. Horses did not stampede the same way that cattle did, maintaining the group formation.

But right now, Dan'l and Snowshoe had other problems. Even as Dan'l watched, the circle of fire closed completely, burning rapidly toward its hub—their camp.

"God's garters!" Snowshoe roared. He rolled out of his robes, cursing like a teamster. "Boone, our bacon is basted!"

"Caulk up, you old fool! Stir up them embers for me!"

"Embers? Ain't this enough goldang fire?"

"Stir 'em, 'shoe, then getcher damn mule hobbled 'fore he bolts into the flames!"

While he issued these terse commands, Dan'l was hastily untying his lineback. Wind whipped fiercely all around them, driving the flames to a crackling, leaping frenzy. Inexorably, the burning circle closed tighter and tighter, a deadly noose.

"We can't ride through it!" Dan'l roared out

above the screaming racket of wind and fire. "It's too wide now, we'd cook getting through it! All we can do is try to start a break-fire and stop it!"

"W'an no damn lightning tonight nohow," Snowshoe declared. " 'At 'ere fire was set, Dan'l!"

"Don't matter a hoot in hell right now what caused it," Dan'l rebuked his friend. "Reach me your powder horn!"

Snowshoe had used his buck knife to stir up the embers of the campfire. Dan'l tugged off one boot. He used it to hastily scoop up the coals.

Dan'l grabbed Snowshoe's powder horn, his own flask, and the boot. Talking to the lineback constantly to calm it, Dan'l grabbed a fistful of mane and swung up onto the dun's bare back.

"Fetch hold of your saddle blanket!" he roared at Snowshoe. Both men were a lurid yellow color in the rapidly advancing flames. "I'm burning a smaller circle around us. Follow me around and let it burn a few feet. Then smother the edges!"

"Ain't no time, Dan'l! We're gone coons!"

Indeed, Dan'l could already feel heat on his skin.

"Stow it, you damned calamity howler! Just do like I said."

It was a close race against time now, and Dan'l knew it all came down to his pony. The lineback dun epitomized the traits Dan'l prized most in a horse: He was a swift dodger, an adept twister, and of good bottom to endure in the face of adversity. How many times had Dan'l bragged to Snowshoe how this lineback could turn on a two-bit piece and give back fifteen cents in change?

Now Dan'l only hoped the dun could live up to these brags.

Dan'l relied on all the dun's power and agility as he went into swift action. First he rode out perhaps fifty yards from their camp, bearing directly toward the heat and smoke. The lineback wanted to bolt, but Dan'l rode low on his neck, speaking into his ear constantly to calm him.

Giant fingers of flame shot at them, forcing the dun to swerve instantly. Riding in a circle, Dan'l halted at regular intervals to shake black powder into the grass. Then, tipping the now-smoldering boot, he ignited each spot with a hot coal. Soon, a curving line of smaller flames leaped in the wind ahead of the bigger fire.

Hobbling crazily on his wooden foot, Snowshoe followed around as best he could and beat out the flames closer to camp. Unfortunately, Dan'l did not have all the time he needed. Nor could he ride close enough to burn the break-fire as wide as he would have liked to. With this wind whipping up, the main fire might leap it and take them anyway.

As the crackling wall of flames pressed ever closer, both men huddled behind their inadequate defense. Dan'l quickly side-lined their pack animals together on short hobbles. Then he hobbled the dun next to Malachi and quickly tied his shirt over its head. Snowshoe did the same with his mule. With the flames out of sight, both animals calmed noticably.

But heat and flames pressed ever closer, driving bitter smoke and snapping sparks before them.

"Think that fire line will hold?" Snowshoe demanded.

"Happens it don't," Dan'l shot back, "we'll be the first to know, old hoss."

Dan'l laughed at that, and Snowshoe scowled, failing to see the humor. Despite his devil-may-have-it grin, however, Dan'l picked up his flintlock pistol and loaded rifle.

Snowshoe understood. He, too, eased his over-and-under pistol from his sash.

If that main fire *did* leap Dan'l's breakline, the two men would each need three final shots: two to kill their mounts and pack animals, one to kill themselves. Even a brave man was wise to choose a bullet over being roasted alive.

There was a sudden upsurge in the wind. A huge, rolling wall of fire closed in on them, so close and so hot that Dan'l felt the liquid drying from his eyeballs.

"Here she comes!" Dan'l roared. "With a bone in her teeth! Cover down, Snowshoe, and may God have mercy on our souls!"

Chapter Four

Widow Maker raised one hand in signal to his companion behind him. River of Blood nudged his pony forward to join him.

"Brother," Widow Maker said, holding his voice just above a whisper. "You have eyes! Only look what we have wrought."

"I have eyes," the Kiowa agreed. "Although it is hard to credit those eyes. Is this a vision placed over them? Not even a dung beetle could have survived that."

It was just past dawn. The two renegades sat their horses atop a low ridge overlooking the fire-ravaged grassland below. In the furry gray light of morning, the sight was eerie and unreal, an image from a fever dream.

The entire range, so far as the naked eye could

see, was charred black. The acrid stink of flames still stained the air. Smoke rose in sinewy blue wisps like fog. Nothing else moved.

"Only hope," Widow Maker said, "that in our hurry, we were not *too* thorough. We need to find enough proof it was Sheltowee we roasted. Charred bones will not secure our trade goods."

"Gilpin told me Boone's weapons have metal plates, etched with his name in the whiteskin talking letters. His silver saddle trimmings, too, are distinctive. And there is a medicine necklace he wears containing the hair of his whiteskin whore. If we sift the ashes, buck, we will find our proof. But careful now. The ground still smolders in places."

Letting their wary mounts set their own pace, the two Indians moved cautiously down the blackened slope. Charred ground crunched like cinders under the horses' hooves.

"The mighty Sheltowee!" Widow Maker shouted with abrupt scorn. "The great Indian slayer! The white-eyed legend whom bullets could not touch. But flames tickled him a bit, eh, Kaitsenko?"

River of Blood laughed outright, a harsh bark of contempt. "Brother, rolling off a log would be more difficult than killing this Daniel Boone. He must—"

The Kiowa was in mid sentence when something caught the corner of his eye—a small circle of grass that had escaped flames. But then, that meant that perhaps Boone—

River of Blood was still forming the unwelcome thought when a little popping sound of primer was followed by the roaring main charge of a flint-lock.

There was a hollow *whup* of impact. A puff of dust rose from the left flank of Widow Maker's favorite war pony, a dappled gray with a blazed face. The battle-experienced rider automatically swung his legs out wide to avoid being trapped as the gray shuddered and collapsed, blowing bloody froth.

A second musket ball took the tip off River of Blood's clan feather. Without words, acting from experience, the big Kiowa offered one hand to his companion. Widow Maker swung up behind him on the buckskin. The double load was heavy, but southwest Indians customarily slit their horses' nostrils to increase their wind and stamina for such emergencies.

Bent low to decrease targets, they fled back up the ridge, a third musket ball nipping at their heels.

"Hell and furies!" Dan'l cursed. "I dropped a good horse instead of a rotten Injun! Well, there's naught else for it, I reckon. Old Patsy Plumb here"—he patted the breech of his flintlock rifle—"is sighted for game at two hundred yards. Them red sons was a mite farther out, and in weak light."

"Why, you blind sonofabitch," Snowshoe teased him. "You couldn't hit a bull in the butt with a banjo!" But Snowshoe immediately grinned and added, "You done good, Dan'l! Now them scum-suckers know we outfoxed their fire! They'll by-god have to *earn* our dander!"

Dan'l scowled as he slid his flintlock back into its saddle boot. "They sent out the first fighter, not us. Now we best put the quietus on them bastards, and do it quick. Else they'll plant us first. I'll wager Stratton has put a good price on our hides."

Despite their good fortune in surviving that inferno, Dan'l was in one hell of a pet. One of his boots was ruined, burnt useless by the hot coals he had carried in it. He was tired, hungry, scratchy-eyed from lack of sleep. And not only were killers on their trail—now Dan'l and Snowshoe would have to hem that mustang band in all over again.

"Well, we'll need to open another water hole and close thissen, seeing how the graze around here is all burned off. But take it by and large," Dan'l said, cheering up a mite, "might've been worse. Leastways we didn't build the catch pen yet."

"Why, right as rain, Boone! Sumbitch woulda burnt down. Well, where you reckon the band'll hole up now?"

Dan'l mulled that while his direct, penetrating gaze swept the lonesome and rough terrain to all sides. "Hard to say. Wild horses have more secrets than tame ones."

Both men knew, without bothering to mention it, that even bears and panther attacks could not upset mustangs like fires could. Poco Loco would drive that bunch far away, perhaps even leave their usual range. It would be the devil's own work to drive them back into the sagebrush flats.

Snowshoe pointed northeast. "How 'bout the bottom woods just off the prairie? Grass all around it, and it's a good place to hide."

Dan'l shook his head. "When you ever see horses hide? They run. Can't run in no woods. 'Sides that, soggy ground ruins a horse's feet. They'll stay nowhere near it."

"Mebbe so, but Poco Loco's got mares near foaling time. Can't run forever. Wherever we pen 'em, they'll need plenty of grass. You seen how weak they get if you close-herd 'em on overgrazed range."

Dan'l nodded. "My guess is they'll push for the dry flats around the Trinity," he decided. "Happens they do, hell, we'll pen 'em right there. Anyhow, even a clabber-lipped greenhorn can read sign behind a hunnert horses. We'll salt their tails quick enough! Let's get thrashing."

As Dan'l had predicted, the broad swath of churned dirt left by the fleeing mustangs led southeast toward the Trinity River. As the new sun rose and burned off the morning haze, the two riders made good time. The only delays were the wide detours to avoid possible ambush points.

Dan'l's eyes scanned constantly, watching for movement and not shape. Mirages were common out here, and shapes could not be trusted.

"By Godfrey!" Snowshoe exclaimed at one point. "Dan'l, I reckon that *was* the Pacer on that ridge. Just look how quick trouble come after we seed it."

"True nuff, hoss. But we don't need to see visions to get our reg'lar rations of trouble."

Even as Dan'l said this, he reined in his dun and

stood up in the stirrups to stare out ahead of them. Snowshoe stared too, shading his eyes with one hand. He shook his head.

"Dan'l, I do believe them eyes of yours can see to next week! This child can't see nothing."

"Quarter your mule around," Dan'l ordered him. "Then look from the side of your eye."

Snowshoe did as told.

"See it now?" Dan'l demanded.

The trapper finally nodded, both red braids of his beard jiggling affirmation. "Someone's coming this way. Plenty of riders. Hell'va dust column risin' up."

Both men watched for a few more minutes.

"There's a coach," Dan'l finally said. And moments later he recognized the distinctive, beetle-backed shape of a reinforced Spanish boullion coach. It was likely loaded with silver *barras* from the mines near Vera Cruz. It would be used to pay soldiers and merchants in the far-north City of the Holy Faith, Santa Fe.

And now both men could also make out several squads of helmeted lancers on well-trained mounts, riding guard on the flanks.

"Just our damned luck, Sheltowee!"

Snowshoe, out of sorts from bad diet and tobacco starvation, loosed a string of foul curses that made Dan'l wince at the blasphemy.

"Mister, have you been baptized?" Dan'l scolded.

"Hell yes! But the water must not a been hot enough, Boone, for it didn't take!"

Perhaps because they were tired and disgusted,

both men laughed hard with reckless abandon—
so hard they nearly slid from their saddles. But
Dan'l had been keeping his gaze on the formation.
He saw one squad of lancers suddenly veer away
from the others and bear toward the two Americans.

Dan'l felt cold fingers squeeze his heart when he
saw it, flapping in the wind: These lancers were
flying the highly feared Black Flag: *Death to all
intruders!*

"Gee up!" he roared out to the lineback, evening
the reins and whacking both heels into the dun's
ribs. "Snowshoe, quitcher gawking, y'unnerstan'?
Them Espanish ain't coming to invite us to a fandango! Make tracks!"

Malachi was fleet-footed for a mule, and for
some time the two men managed to keep their
present distance from the dogged lancers. Dan'l
could feel the dun's heart thumping against his
legs, strong as a Mohawk war drum.

But these Spanish mounts were fresh and recently grained. The interval between hunter and
prey steadily shrank.

Dan'l halted with a shout and wheeled his pony
around, leaping down. "Grab hold my reins,
Snowshoe! Time to make these fish-eaters ease
off."

In open country like this, Dan'l always made
sure he carried two pointed sticks in his saddle
pouch. Now he jammed both sticks into the
ground, slanting one over the other in an *X* to
form rifle cross-sticks. Dan'l shook a double load
into his frizzen—two hundred grains of black

powder, a "buffalo load." Then he twisted the breech plug open, thumbing a half-ounce ball behind the loading gate.

"You're just washing bricks, Sheltowee!" Snowshoe scoffed. "They're too far out! That exter powder, she'll give you the range. But you'll lose your aim."

"Shut your cake-hole," Dan'l ordered as he took scant cover behind a fold in the ground and rested his muzzle on the cross-sticks. "Only thing pullin' me off bead is all your damned frettin'!"

The riders—over a dozen strong—thundered closer, yellow-brown dust columns boiling up behind them. Dan'l squinted against the distance as he took up his trigger slack. The flintlock bucked into his shoulder; an eyeblink later, the lead lancer threw two surprised arms toward heaven, then rolled almost gracefully off the back of his horse. He bounced for a second like a human tumbleweed.

"Target!" Snowshoe roared out. "That's Kentucky windage, Boone!"

Both men loosed a raucous cheer. But it immediately died on their lips as they saw what happened next.

Instead of turning back, or even halting, these well-trained veterans simply ignored the dead man and divided into pairs at wide intervals. Never missing a pace, they continued to hurtle toward the two surprised long hunters.

"Well, I'm a Dutchman!" Dan'l grabbed his reins from Snowshoe and hit leather, wheeling his pony for the run. He snubbed the pack horse's leadline so it would be forced to keep up or choke.

"Naught else for it, hoss!" Dan'l added. "The band'll wait! There ain't even enough cover out here to hide our thoughts behind, let alone us and these animals. Sugar-talk that damn mule, Snowshoe, or damn soon now we'll be looking up to see daisies!"

Chapter Five

"Boone will *never* drive a herd over that desert," scoffed Lev Vogel's head lackey, a fellow Russian trapper named Nikolai Bulgakov. "Apaches out there call it the Devil's Floor. The Spaniard Oñate tried to cross it with ten excellent herders and only thirty animals. Between Indians, rough weather, and drought, he lost every horse."

Vogel listened quietly to this, nodding when Bulgakov fell silent. "You're right, Nika. Oñate said the Cimarron Desert alone is almost two hundred miles without a drop of water."

Vogel flashed his lips-only smile as he stabbed his heel into a bootjack and tugged off a boot. "But never forget," he reminded his companion, "that Daniel Boone measures grain by his own bushel! Such men cover a great distance while other men are voting whether to start today or tomorrow. People said he'd never survive the Cumberland Gap all winter, but he did. And people said he'd never escape from his Indian captors up in Detroit, but he did that, too. People were just wrong. They fail to understand that Boone is not one of the many."

Vogel fell silent and finished running a bore patch through the single barrel of an ornate Bohemian flintlock pistol. The two men squatted by their gear in the light of a roaring squad fire. Vogel had ordered his men to camp for the night in a rain-washed meadow near the Georgia Colony's Savannah River. They had been heading west for three days now.

"All right, suppose Boone does manage to somehow reach the Colbert with horses," Bulgakov said. He used the old French name for the Mississippi River. "They'll never swim those currents. I've seen barges caught like corks in a torrent. He'll need to use the old ferry at Frenchman's Lick. You've seen that country, Lev. Flat and open. It would be what these local rubes call a turkey shoot."

Vogel laughed outright. Both men were former Cossacks and did not shy away from bluntness. Vogel said, "I told you what Stratton said. He seems convinced Boone will die out west. Stratton swears this is a two-try plan, and *we're* the second try. If he's right, we'll go fishing and still draw wages. Stratton is good for it."

All around the two men, Vogel's minions had gathered in small groups to cook "ramrod bread"

over small fires—cornmeal plastered to the bayonets on their rifles. Some had constructed small
brush shelters for the night.

Vogel said, "Killing Boone would obviously be
of great personal satisfaction. But bear in mind—
it's any *horses* Boone might be driving that Stratton fears most. And horses are an easy target, even
if Boone isn't."

Sha-hee-ka, cramped behind a fallen log only fifteen feet behind Vogel, clearly overheard his
words.

So that was their game. Lansford Stratton had
resumed his favorite campaign: the battle to destroy Daniel Boone and everything he stood for.
It was Tory and Rebel, locked in their battle for
the future of this continent.

So it was not to be a Cherokee battle after all,
as she had feared. Except, she reasoned, in this:
Any victory by a dangerous man like Stratton
spelled woe for the red man. Never mind that her
own father was British. Never mind that Cherokees were legally subjects of King George. To
Stratton, all Indians were aboriginal savages without souls.

Her muscles ached and protested from being
locked in one position for so long. For days now
Sha-hee-ka had paddled her flat-bottomed bateau
along the Savannah River, tracking Vogel's private army of frontier scavengers and criminals. A
few Russians, some Germans and Dutch, a few
Frenchmen—the dregs of their respective nations.

So far they had stuck to the Continental toll

road beside the river. She could see them now dotting the little meadow like fungi. About two dozen strong, each man with a full, if sometimes shoddy battle rig and a string of two to six horses. It had taken Sha-hee-ka hours, beginning just before sunset, to inch into her present position.

But she was hardly safe. Imagination wove a horrid scenario of what would happen if even one man spotted her. She knew they would all "take her out on the prairie"—line up and take turns bulling her before they tortured her to death. And even if she was not discovered, one of those scouts constantly coming and going could easily find her bateau hidden nearby.

Again she glanced at the Russian named Vogel and shivered a bit at the livid comma formed by the dueling scar on his right cheek; she glanced, too, at the eyes as lifeless as two dried seeds. No better word could be spoken of a man than that he was careful of his horses. Yet earlier she had watched Vogel fly into a rage when his big bay refused to take the bit. Vogel had beaten the horse mercilessly in the head with a rope and picket pin, drawing blood.

She knew him as a quiet and brooding man, a dangerous man who could act on murderous impulse before thinking. And a treacherous man— one who did not scruple to leave bullet holes in a man's back.

Daniel Boone, Sha-hee-ka decided, was too much man for the likes of Vogel to kill. But even two dozen drunk Choctaws could easily slaughter a band of ponies trapped in the open.

Sha-hee-ka knew Boone and admired him. But she wasn't sure that even he could actually reach the Mississippi with a herd of Western scrubs. But the plucky Kaintuck explorer, though hardly a Cherokee ally, was a far better man than Stratton or his lickspittles.

Despite the risks, Sha-hee-ka decided to see this fight through. She was a War Woman, sworn to serve the Warrior Way in the quest for justice. But this would not be an easy battle. She was alone, hungry, tired, and ill-equipped. One slip and she was trapped in the lion's den.

She *must* stay awake. Sha-hee-ka removed some tobacco leaves from her parfleche and chewed them until she had a little juice. This she smeared inside her eyelids. It was an old Cherokee trick—the mild stinging was harmless, but would last for hours and help keep her alert.

The ground was wet and cold, and Sha-hee-ka had only a doeskin shirt against its seeping dampness. Chiggers dug at her legs. Somebody sang a drunken song in Russian. Sha-hee-ka asked the High Holy Ones to make her strong and brave, to help her remember that courage was better than comfort.

With courage, she would face Death the way Daniel Boone always did: with weapons to hand and a mocking grin.

Dan'l Boone was not grinning, however, when even his expert marksmanship failed to slow those dogged Spanish lancers.

A wild horse depended on running away from

predators as its chief defense. These wide-open spaces were ideal for keeping an enemy in constant sight. But Dan'l also knew that he and Snowshoe were about to be doomed by that same wide-open vastness.

Nature, however, intervened abruptly, and Dan'l wasted no time seizing the moment.

The lancers had closed to within shouting distance, and the gap was narrowing. Abruptly, a violent southwest dust storm—a giant whirling dervish—whipped up quick as scat across the flats.

Desperately, Dan'l tracked its erratic progress, trying to get a fix on the boiling, yellow-brown column. Then, shouting at Snowshoe above the racket, he signaled a turn in the same direction as the dust storm.

It was a defensive maneuver Dan'l had learned from watching southwest Papago Indians, who called it "quartering the wind." He and Snowshoe continued to track diagonally across the funnel's path. Thus, they stayed ahead of it, yet constantly forced their pursuers to ride directly into it. Soon, even the tenacious lancers could not abide this choking maelstrom. They abandoned their pursuit and returned to the coach.

Dan'l and Snowshoe finally reached some caliche hills and rested there for a few hours in a wind-sheltered cutbank. Dan'l watched Snowshoe and his mule share the last of their mescal from Snowshoe's limp hat. Both men were hungry and thirsty, but that would have to wait. First priority was picking up the trail of that *manada*. The next priority was to get a catch pen built and trap the mustangs so they could be broken.

They found Poco Loco and his band exactly where Dan'l predicted they would: grazing the bunchgrass flats near the Trinity River. Several were rolling on the ground, bathing in sand to wash off the sweat of their recent panic run.

"Poco Loco got most of 'em bunched again," Dan'l observed. "Well, we best not go any closer just yet."

He halted his dun on a low rise well back from the mustangs. "Horses stay skittish for days after a hard stampede. We could set 'em off again in a finger-snap. Just a cough or a slicker rustling could do it. We'll make a meat camp, get some rest."

"*Meat* camp!" Snowshoe groused. "Air ye daft, Boone? Mayhap we'll kill a rattler. Elsewise, it's river-water soup and air pudding for *these* coons!"

Dan'l's strong white teeth flashed through his beard when he grinned. "Hoss, I told you my rule when it comes to mustanging."

"Yes, damnit. Only take bachelors."

"No, the other one: Take no man who can't eat horse meat. For that's what's on the spit for supper, old son. We hide out and shoot the spy Poco Loco sends back."

Snowshoe turned a shade pale, but made no protest. He was too damned hungry. Both men watched the *manada* below—or most of it, for a few had been lost or killed in the recent flight.

"We'll let 'em get used to seeing us out here," Dan'l said. "Malachi's got a case on that little *grullo* mare. So when we start to move closer, we'll send Malachi out on point."

Snowshoe nodded at the wisdom of this. Stallions tolerated mules, for they were able to sense that mules, like geldings, were not competing for the mares.

"We can build the catch pen right near here," Dan'l decided. "Plenty of good lumber and brush for the wings."

"We taking mares too?" Snowshoe demanded.

Dan'l nodded. They would be needed for breeding back east, where none of these wild horses were yet being bred. He knew there was a powerful bias, at least among white men, against riding mares. But it was tarnal foolishness. Dan'l knew mares to be enduring and brave, and much more trustworthy as camp animals.

"We take the mares," he said. "But no animals under thirteen hands. And once we pen 'em, we got to hire on a few local Injuns as bronco busters. Take them hours to do what takes us days."

"That shines right," Snowshoe agreed. His eyes swept the scant-grown hills all around them. "But you tell me something, wise Mr. Boone."

"The hell you waitin' on—you got a bone in your throat?"

"Just this," Snowshoe said. "Where's them two blanket asses that tried to roast us alive?"

Dan'l shrugged. "How long is a piece of string? Reckon we'll find out where they are next time they try to kill us."

57

Chapter Six

"Look at them!" Widow Maker spat with contempt. "These hair-faced intruders come into our ranges preaching the superiority of their odd ways. *Their* ways? This pen they are building to steal *our* horses—they learned of it from your people, brother!"

"As you say." River of Blood nodded. He didn't bother to point out, however, that his Kiowa tribe had in turn stolen the trick from the Spanish—making it originally the white man's, after all.

The two renegades had taken cover on a timbered ridge west of the Spanish mirror station at Carrizo Springs. For three full sleeps now they had watched Boone and his red-bearded companion at work beside the Trinity River. The two white men had so far allowed no further opportunity for ambush.

These whiteskins, both Indians reluctantly agreed, were impressive frontiersmen who knew exactly what they were doing. Location was critical in penning wild horses. Boone and his companion carefully selected a brushy hollow in a canyon, a spot near the riverbank where the herd often crossed. And Boone had wisely placed the gate so it faced the southwest. Obviously he knew that running horses raised so much dust it would blow ahead of them and disguise the gate.

The pen itself was crude, but strong. Using axes and an adze, the two whites felled nearby trees and made sturdy boards for the sides. But the essential feature was the long wings that flared out from the gate to form a huge *V*. These were disguised with brush. Running horses would avoid touching anything, so the narrowing wings would gradually funnel them into the pen.

"They even know about sham wings," River of Blood pointed out.

He nodded in the direction of the braided-beard with the wooden foot. The burly white man had fashioned a crude plow out of leather straps and a pointed branch. Rigging it to his mule, he had plowed two lines out from the ends of the brush wings. In effect, this extended the *V* even wider. Wild horses feared a dark line of unsodded earth, and would not cross over it.

Widow Maker, too, was impressed by all this.

But his hair-trigger temper made him swear impatiently in Spanish.

"*Maldita!* No more of this spying and hand-wringing, Kaitsenko! So Boone escaped from a prairie fire—old women have done the same! That 'legend' killed my best war horse. I would rather be scalped by the Wendigos than live any longer with this insult."

Widow Maker turned from the sight below to stare at the two horses tethered behind him and River of Blood, gnawing tree bark as Indian ponies often did. The dappled gray Boone killed had been Widow Maker's prize possession. The Comanche stole it from an Apache chieftain during a raid into the Gila River country.

But Widow Maker had many fine ponies on his string. He had returned to the Comanche camp at Blanco Canyon and cut a worthy replacement out from the common corral: a *canelo* or cinnamon, a light and strong red roan with nervous ears and intelligent eyes.

"That is a mean horse," River of Blood said, watching his companion's eyes appraise the *canelo*.

Widow Maker nodded. The little bow-legged Comanche's ears were pierced with small brass rings. "He is mean. Nor did I break him of the habit after I captured him. I have watched Boone on this ugly coyote dun of his. It is a good horse, and Boone is a good rider. But before Sister Sun moves the width of two lodge poles, I will prove that good is not enough against a Comanche."

*   *   *

"A man's backbone has to give and take," Dan'l said. "Especially at the tail. Elsewise, he'll never be a horseman."

Dan'l sleeved sweat off his forehead as he made this observation. Snowshoe nudged his mule up until he was beside Dan'l.

"We ain't horses *nor* men, Boone," he grumped. "Just goldang jackasses. My sitter's fair ready to fall off! I say we rest a spell."

"All that's wearing your sitter out," Dan'l said, swinging down from the saddle, "is the same damned rhythm over and over. Rest, hell! A new gait means a fresh ride! We'll trade off a spell."

The two men traded mounts, Snowshoe still cursing like a stable sergeant. Poco Loco and his *manada*, likewise worn out, had stopped to graze about five hundred yards ahead. But Dan'l didn't plan to let them rest long.

He and Snowshoe were deliberately running the band on hard ground, both to wear the fight out of them and to make them tender-footed—and thus, less likely to run on their own. All the other work was done. First the two had inspected the Trinity River for quicksand bars before erecting their catch pen nearby. Then had come this final running of the mustangs to exhaust them—fresh horses were nearly impossible to pen.

Malachi, still love-struck for the blue mare, tried to run forward and join the wild horses. Dan'l held him back by dint of sheer muscle.

"We ain't careful," Dan'l said, recalling the Pacing White Mustang, "our stock will turn mustang."

Dan'l had seen it, even in the eyes of his dun—

some trace memory of his days in the wilderness, unfettered by men and bridles.

"We best be careful, awright," Snowshoe said. "But not jist for our mounts. Whoever tried to do for us has been tracking us like cats on rats. 'Em 'ere savages is about to make another play."

"That's the way of it," Dan'l agreed. He snapped Malachi's reins. "Gee up! Let's wheel the herd, old son, and run 'em hard one last time."

Shouting and yipping, the two friends again prodded the reluctant horses into motion, many of them limping slightly by now. Dan'l had learned about these horses from close observation during two sojourns in the southwest country. Spanish stock walked slow and trotted hard, but had a smooth, soft gallop.

And it was a gallop that Dan'l pushed them to now, long manes and tails flapping like lance streamers. It was finally time, Dan'l decided, to pen these magnificent animals.

While they let the band settle down, Dan'l and Snowshoe made a grass fire and smoked their skin and clothing to blunt the human scent.

"Move slow and steady from here on out," Dan'l told Snowshoe quietly. "Happens we spook Poco Loco, tender feet won't stop 'em. We'll get nothing but their dust."

The mustangs were grazing only a few hundred yards from the brush-disguised pen. Dan'l had a plan. If it worked, he and Snowshoe would own a herd of horses before the sun went down.

"Snowshoe, I want you hid good in the brush.

Soon as the last of the band goes inside, hook that gate shut quick. *Don't* get caught in it if they mill, just let 'em get away. They'll trample you to paste."

Snowshoe flicked nervous eyes toward the timbered ridges to their west. "Trample a cat's tail, Boone! It's dry-gulching savages givin' me the fantods. Once we got our eyes locked on them critters, 'em red bastards mean to pounce."

Dan'l laughed loud and hard. "One world at a time, nervous Nellie! Hell, worst can happen is you'll get yourself kilt. You afraid to get your life over? Why, most fellas live too long, anyhow."

"Boone, I swan! You ain't quite right in your upper story!"

"Crazy as a loon, I am!" Dan'l agreed heartily. "Crazy-by-thunder, a wild man! Now quitcher damn puling, hoss. We got mustangs to pen."

Moving slowly, Dan'l unsaddled one of their packhorses—a swayback pinto they called Yankee Noodle—and stripped it of its neck leather. He began leading it into the pen.

"It'll never work, Boone," Snowshoe carped. "Not by a jugful."

"Shush it, calamity howler. Will too. That little blue mare has got her eye on this old plug. And Poco Loco don't like it one damn bit."

Dan'l's plan to pen the wild horses depended on the fact that stallions were not only polygamous, but also jealously guarded their mares. But Dan'l didn't want to go too far and enrage Poco Loco. Few men realized it, but a savage stallion—once blood was in its eyes—was the most dangerous creature on four legs.

Dan'l stopped just inside the pen and hid behind Yankee Noodle. Dan'l was an expert at imitating many animal sounds. Now he unleashed a convincing neigh that made the mustangs lift their heads, ears pricked forward.

Again Dan'l made the noise. It worked—the little *grullo* mare was trotting closer. Poco Loco, busy bunching the herd, hadn't yet noticed. But Dan'l knew he soon would, and the racket he'd make would wake snakes.

Leaving the packhorse hobbled where it was, Dan'l ran to the far side of the pen and slipped out between the boards. He limped almost as badly as Snowshoe, for Dan'l had repaired his burned boot with only a flap of rawhide and some sinew stitches—hardly fancy work.

His lineback dun waited nearby, saddled and ready. It was a homely little four-year-old—nothing special, Dan'l always said modestly, just a good little pony to ride the river with.

The blue mare cautiously entered the sham wings, then the wings; finally Poco Loco looked up and saw her, approaching Yankee Noodle. Whinnying his rage, rearing high in his wrath, the master stallion raced toward the pen.

Now Dan'l had to make his move, and he had to time it just right. The band, if spooked but not actually panicked by fire or panthers, would automatically run to bunch around Poco Loco. Which meant Dan'l had to haze them while the stallion was inside the pen, using the mass of them to block Poco Loco's escape. Timing would be critical—including the precise moment when Snow-shoe had to secure that gate.

Snowshoe sounded the owl hoot when Poco Loco was inside. Abruptly, Dan'l heeled his dun in the flanks hard and discharged both barrels of his pistol, startling the band.

Yipping, slapping his dun with his hat, Dan'l funneled the bunch forward. His dun twisted and dodged like a cattle dog. It went off without a hitch. Before Poco Loco could wheel and lead his favorite mare out, the main gather of the band were on them. As the last wide-eyed animals dashed inside, a triumphant Snowshoe slammed the corral gate closed and looped it shut.

"We done 'er, Boone! Folks said it would be eas-ier to catch a weasel asleep, but we by God done 'er! We got us a herd!"

Dan'l grinned and raised his left hand high to salute his companion's fast work. An eyeblink later, Dan'l roared like a wounded bear—a quartz-tipped lance had just punched into his upraised hand, ripping through the web of flesh at the base of his thumb.

Hellfire leaped down his arm. Dan'l reached up, snapped off the light reed lance, drove the shaft through his hand clean. But when he looked up, his useless hand already swelling, the big explorer realized his troubles had just begun: A wild-eyed Comanche, face greased for battle, was closing in on him at a gallop, a bow in one hand, a fistful of arrows in the other!

Chapter Seven

It took Dan'l only a few moments to realize that this Comanche was attacking alone. Dan'l understood immediately: It was a revenge match for that pony he'd killed.

Damn prideful redskins, he cursed. Hell, this was no time for a set-to. His left hand was swollen—stove up so bad he could hardly form a claw with it. But at least blood loss was minimal. It hurt like the devil, but he could tend to it later. Assuming he was still alive.

That was Dan'l's final grim thought as he reined his lineback around to meet the attack. His eyes sought Snowshoe's position. The trapper should have had a clear line of fire at the attacking Indian. But quick as a heartbeat, Dan'l felt his blood turn to slush when he saw his friend's dilemma.

66

Terror-stricken mustangs had bulged the gate and somehow released the loop securing it. Now Snowshoe, muscles straining like taut guy lines, held the gate shut by hand. If he let go even for a moment to help Dan'l, there went the herd!

"You stay right there, hoss!" Dan'l bellowed. "*I'll* settle this featherhead's hash!"

However, Dan'l's reckless boast belied the obvious skill of this Comanche killing machine now hurtling toward him. Dan'l knew the Comanches were called the natural jockeys of the Plains, and he had heard marvelous tales of their highly feared horsemanship. A Comanche on foot, it was said, was bow-legged and awkward, lacking in confidence; but once mounted on his war pony, he was trouble off its leash.

And those tales were all true, Dan'l saw now. This Comanche did not even appear to be riding his pony. Rather, he seemed a natural extension of it. He bounced along without even gripping, either with knees or hands, in a perfect rhythm with his animal. This left both hands free to string and fire arrows, which he did with a deadly precision.

Arrows whiffed and hummed all about his ears as Dan'l deftly twisted his little dun in evasive patterns. He managed to avoid that first deadly flurry, but the Comanche was still attacking at full speed. And he was already tugging another handful of arrows from a coyoteskin quiver.

Using his good arm, Dan'l freed his long gun from the saddle boot. He slung it up into the off-hand position and steadied the muzzle on his left forearm. The rifle bucked into his shoulder as

Dan'l pulled the trigger, but the graceful Indian warrior had easily twisted out of harm's way.

Recharging his piece was pointless. The Indian could string and shoot ten arrows while Dan'l charged his flintlock once. Nor would his short-gun be any use at this range.

"*Hi-ya!*" Dan'l shouted as he jerked the dun's reins hard right. "Hiii-*ya!*"

It became a riding contest, and although Dan'l was scrambling harder, the scrappy little dun was giving the Comanche's roan a good fight. Constantly twisting, turning, feinting, the lineback proved its own *brío escondido*—hidden vigor.

"Snub your rein, Dan boy!" Snowshoe shouted encouragement. "Hold tight rein, Boone! Make that red bastard work for it!"

The Comanche's last arrow whiffed past Dan'l's cheek, so close the fletching drew a thin, hot line of blood. Never hesitating a moment, his painted face rigid with the killing need, the brave slid his deadly "skull cracker" from its sling—a stone war club, the favorite Comanche weapon when closing for a kill on horseback.

Now the flea-bit bastard is getting into short-gun range, Dan'l thought. He dropped his long gun into the boot and slid his flintlock pistol from its holster. But Dan'l's useless left hand could not grip the reins tight. And the Comanche's amazing *canelo* pony permitted no clear target.

Fighting hard for balance, Dan'l could neither draw a steady bead nor accurately lead his shot—the Indian pony's deft movements were utterly unpredictable. It was like trying to catch a fly with tongs.

"Wheel and draw him off, Dan'l!" Snowshoe bellowed above the thudding, screaming racket of terrified horses. "Meet him on your terms, not his!"

Snowshoe was right, Dan'l realized. He had to outfox this superior rider—not charge straight into the jaws of sure death, British-infantry style.

Dan'l fired one load, but the shot missed. Just as the attacking brave was on the verge of braining him, Dan'l urged the dun to pivot half-right. Dan'l felt the wind from the club as it parted his flying hair. But it missed, and the surprised Comanche— braced in the stirrups for a hard blow—damn near twisted out of his saddle.

Dan'l felt his blood singing with elation. Even this excellent horseman was vulnerable to good strategy.

He raised his pistol to discharge the second barrel. A split second later, Dan'l's hopes were literally sent crashing when the dun's right foreleg plunged into a badger hole. Dan'l's teeth jarred in his skull when he smashed into the hard ground, almost blacking out.

Dan'l lay still for a few critical seconds, his mind coming round slow, like a cold snake waking up.

Dan'l! Dan'l Boone! Goddamnit, Sheltowee, get up!

Dan'l heard Snowshoe's voice as if it were muffled by thick banks of fog. The hard ground trembled under him, approaching hooves pounding a rat-a-tat-tat rhythm of death.

Dan'l! Up on the line!

Dan'l's eyes snapped open, he sat up. His dun, limping but not seriously hurt, trotted back toward him. Snowshoe had managed to jam the pen gate shut with a pointed stake. Now he was racing toward his long gun, propped against the side of the corral.

But Dan'l saw clearly that he'd never reach his gun in time to stop this charging savage. Nor could Dan'l possibly get mounted in time. In fact, he barely managed to gain his feet before the Comanche—teeth bared in a triumphant grin—was again looming over him, skull cracker held high.

Dan'l could leap aside, but that would only delay his troubles. So the big frontiersman decided to take the bull by the horns.

It was an old battle trick, perfected by unmounted Indians as a defense against Spanish horsemen. At the last moment, instead of falling away from the charging horse, Dan'l fell in front of its forelegs. But he didn't drop to the ground—he wrapped himself tight around the right leg, gripping for dear life.

It worked. The mustang came crashing down, sending the Comanche flying ears-over-applecart. Dan'l managed to jackknife his body out from under the falling horse. But momentum sent him rolling hard, and there was a bright orange starburst when his skull banged into a twisted palo duro.

This time Dan'l didn't black out, but his limbs went numb and tingly, and he couldn't move. Thank the good lord, it didn't matter—Dan'l watched Snowshoe finally snatch up his long iron. The Comanche, badly shaken himself, barely managed to catch up his pony and escape.

"You alive, Boone?" Snowshoe demanded, sounding doubtful as he limped closer. "By Godfrey, you got enough guts to fill a smokehouse! Sheltowee, you *wrassled* that pony down, you farmer's bull! That damn Comanch got the little end of the horn that time!"

Dan'l shook his head, sat up, and gingerly inventoried his bones with his good hand. "That was some pumpkins, wunnit?" he finally boasted when he realized he was still in one piece.

But Dan'l's elation was tempered by the memory of that ugly Comanche's determined face. No doubt Lansford Stratton and Hugh Gilpin had started all this trouble with bribes.

But now it was personal, a grudge fight. And it wouldn't be over until either the red men went to their funeral scaffolds or the white men went to their graves.

With his left hand useless while it mended, Dan'l knew those penned broncos would never get broke to leather without help. Nor could two men hope to control a hundred animals all the way to the Mississippi. So he and Snowshoe scoured the country, hoping to hire on a few local tribesmen.

There was constant trouble from Poco Loco, who wanted no part of being a captive. One day after the master stallion was captured, he managed to kick boards loose from the pen.

"Should we clog that sonofabitch?" Snowshoe

suggested. "I got a busted trace we can use."

Dan'l thought about it, then shook his head. Some men clogged wild stallions—strapped a piece of chain to a front ankle—to make them tractable.

"It hinders 'em in a fight with wolves and such," Dan'l said. "And happens he should escape, he could drown at a ford."

"So damn what?" Snowshoe snapped peevishly. Lord God, but he was sick of this damn expedition and wanted nothing but a whorehouse in New Orleans. "Dan'l, you mollycoddle a horse somethin' awful."

Snowshoe was chewing on red-willow bark, unable to pretend it was good Kentucky plug.

"No alcohol," he groused. "No 'baccy, no sugar for my tea. But that don't matter, Christians, cuz I have no damned tea, neither!"

"Yarrow root makes a fine tea," Dan'l suggested.

"Boone, you can stick that arrow root where the sun don't shine! Mister, we can't even pause to think without we got Innuns tryin' to take our hair. Boone, have you *ever* made two bits the easy way?"

"Ahh, shut your fish-trap, you stinkin' old goat. Pile on the agony, it don't matter. Them ponies'll fetch two years wages back in the settlements. All the matter with you is, you need a good whipping. Now let's go hire on some bronco busters."

Men could say what they wanted to about savages. Dan'l had freed more than one from his soul. But he had yet to meet any men who prized horses more or worked them better. He'd even known of

Indians to sleep with their best horse tied to their wrists. No Indian ever sold a good war horse, and neither did Dan'l Boone.

Within two days, they managed to find three Papago Indians willing to work for wampum beads and trade goods. But when they showed up for work, they brought along a fourth Indian: a huge, broad-shouldered Mescalero named Grayeyes. He had drifted east from the blazing *jornadas* of the vast country known as Apacheria.

"I ain't so sure 'bout this 'pache," Dan'l told Snowshoe. "I hear tell how 'paches set much store by horse meat. I hear they'll even choose it over any other meat."

"God's truth," Snowshoe confirmed. "Part they like best is that thick, fleshy bit on the neck. Out south of Taos, me and Jeb Rault come across a range covered with dead horses. All missing only that one piece, my hand to Jesus!"

Dan'l translated his objection into halting Spanish, using sign talk when he couldn't think of the right words.

All four Indians grinned when they understood, the Apache especially. The small and wiry Papagos wore loose cotton clothing, thick rope sandals, and wide-brimmed leather hats. The bigger Apache was wrapped in a brightly striped Saltillo blanket from Mexico. Dan'l knew his tribe terrorized the roads of Sonora just as the Comanches terrorized those of Chihuahua.

Grayeyes surprised both men by answering in English. "Fat colts more better than beef, uh?"

The brave glanced over at Malachi, busy swish-

73

ing away flies with his tail. "*Mulas* good fixens too, uh? *Mmm!*"

This brashness coaxed a laugh out of Dan'l, who liked Grayeyes instantly. Snowshoe, however, frowned so deep that his eyebrows touched. "You eat that mule, buck, I'll flay your damn soles."

"If this Apache may not go," one of the Papagos told Dan'l in Spanish, "*we* may not go. Once, he touched a white buffalo. Now he has strong medicine."

"Course he did," Dan'l replied sarcastically. " 'Bout the same time I shaved King George."

But the frontiersman knew it was no use arguing. The white buffalo was venerated by every tribe Dan'l knew of. Any man who touched one, or even sincerely claimed he had, was revered.

Then again, thought Dan'l, maybe he had touched one. How many would believe that he and Snowshoe had spotted the legendary Pacing White Mustang, if they tried to make that claim in a tavern back east?

"Ain't no time to chew it fine," Dan'l told Snowshoe. "We got to gentle them scrubs and make tracks east. Happens Grayeyes cooks a horse or two, we can afford it. I got youngens I'm hankerin' to see before they forget their paw's face."

Snowshoe spat chewed bark into the dirt. "Your ugly face ain't no loss to man nor child. But I'm with you, Sheltowee. The sooner we get shut of this country, the quicker this coon can cheek some chaw. Let's put these red arabs to work!"

Chapter Eight

Sha-hee-ka paused in the moonlit darkness, feeling the presence of death like a man beside her.

In fact, death was many men beside her—perhaps two dozen, scattered around a copse surrounded by tall oak trees dripping streamers of Spanish moss. Lev Vogel's mercenary army was now camped only about a hundred miles northeast of the Mississippi River town of Natchez.

Laughter and curses reached her ears, born on the humid wind along with the steady insect hum and the deep-throated chorus of frogs. Sha-hee-ka timed her movements so that wind gusts covered the noise as she crept ever closer to a crude rope corral.

She knew precisely where Vogel and his cutthroats were heading: to the big riverbend just above Natchez, an old trading post called Frenchman's Lick. The only dependable ferry in this entire region operated there, owned by "Uncle Dick" Macgratten. Even Dan'l Boone could not get a herd of horses across the Mississippi's wide, strong channel without floating them—otherwise, they would be swept out into the Gulf, their bones picked clean by sea scavengers.

So Boone would use Dick's Ferry. And the area around the ferry, still a simple settlement, would become a slaughter ground. Hidden in the dense trees on the east bank of the river, marksmen would have easy targets. The west bank was clear, flat, and open for miles at that point.

Sha-hee-ka had ridden with Boone once against Stratton's treachery at Fort Destiny. And she was not about to desert Boone now. So instead of going on ahead to Frenchman's Lick, she remained behind to sabotage Vogel's mission in whatever ways possible.

Sha-hee-ka had noticed that these men did not share the Cherokee tribe's enthusiasm for war. Rather, morale in this group of thieves and thugs was always hanging by a thread. One way Vogel and his favorite lieutenant, Nikolai Bulgakov, maintained control was with bribes. These included generous rations of rum. Cut off that flow, and mutiny might threaten. At the very least, fighting spirit would be weakened.

Sha-hee-ka slid an obsidian knife from a beaded sheath on her sash. Moving swift and silent like a shadow, she slipped under the rope and into the corral. She had already spent hours deliberately exposing the stock to her smell; now they hardly stirred as she slipped in among them, making little soothing sounds.

Heart pounding against her ribs, Sha-hee-ka located a sorrel packhorse laden with a huge gutbag of liquor. The squad pails were drawn from this each evening after the last meal was cooked. Sha-hee-ka made a small, ragged hole—big enough to drain the bag soon, yet uneven enough to look like an accidental rip.

Sha-hee-ka was about to retreat back to her bateau when a stick snapped behind her.

Fear jolted her like a mule kick. She whirled and found herself only inches away from a likewise startled mercenary. He, too, had crept up to the corral—and the gourd cup in his hand explained why. Either his regular ration wasn't enough, or he had been cut off as punishment.

His startled eyes feasted on the dark-haired, comely half-breed—the flat, clay-colored plane of her stomach, the ample breasts, the heart-shaped lips.

"Mon dieu!" the Frenchman exclaimed. "And what are *you* up to, eh, *ma jolie?"*

But his "little pretty" did not bother to answer this idiotic question. Nor did the Cherokee War Woman waste time debating her next move. At times, thought could kill you. If this man let out a shout now, she was worm fodder. And that meant Daniel Boone would soon join her.

The hardcase swore, for he had just noticed liquor streaming from the gut-bag. "What are you—?"

Sha-hee-ka had performed this kill before: one silent, hard, well-placed thrust precisely between the fourth and fifth ribs. That way, it was straight into the heart.

Heat flooded her hand and wrist as the blade penetrated deep into vitals. Sha-hee-ka actually felt the final heartbeats, transmitted up the stone knife to her hand. The mercenary shuddered like a gut-hooked fish, then folded dead to the ground.

"Armand?" a voice demanded out of the surrounding shadows. "Armand, hurry on, you fool! Lev will shave our heads if he catches us!"

Footsteps approached, and Sha-hee-ka willed her nerves steady. So much for the element of surprise—now Vogel would be alerted to her presence. Best to clear out quick, and take up a position near Dick's Ferry.

If only she knew what route Boone was taking, she could ford the river and ride on to warn him. But she would have to settle for trying to warn him when he reached Frenchman's Lick. Assuming she could elude capture that long.

As she crept away through the trees and brush, Sha-hee-ka reminded herself that odds were good that Boone wouldn't make it with a herd, anyway. In that case there was no good reason for him to use Dick's Ferry, which was expensive. It was primarily a wagon ferry and freighting station. So Sha-hee-ka found herself praying that, for once, the mighty Sheltowee failed.

Success, this time, might very well kill him.

*　　*　　*

"Set 'em to work!" Snowshoe had exclaimed of the Indian bronco busters, despite the threat from hidden killers. So for the next few days, work went on "from can to can't," in Dan'l's wry phrase.

If there was harder work anywhere on God's green earth than gentling wild horses, Dan'l had yet to learn of it. It was a job that could literally shake a man to death. Once, in Old Mexico, Dan'l watched a bronc buster step off a horse, slap at his chaps, take three steps, then drop dead on the spot.

Although the two palefaces were less adept at it, they too pitched in, observing closely and learning from the Indians. Dan'l's hand mended slowly and hampered him, while Snowshoe was too damned impatient.

But the three wiry Papagos—two of them twin brothers named Buffalo Runner and Coyote Man, the third their older uncle, Guadalupe—were top hands by any reckoning. The twins were annoying practical jokers and big eaters with hollow legs, but strong and enduring. Their Uncle Guadalupe was dour and leather-faced, always cursing in Spanish, but a first-rate worker, Dan'l noticed, as was Grayeyes, the big, horse-eating Apache whom Snowshoe fully mistrusted.

The roping technique known farther south as "lassoing" was still widely unknown in the north; it was practiced among only a few Mexican vaqueros or Argentine gauchos. Dan'l's fire would be well banked before such roping became a common skill on the American frontier. For now, he and Snowshoe snared each pony by employing the ingenious Indian method of their day.

They held their loops open by tying them to light rings made of willow switches. Holding the ring in their hands, they had to ride up until even with a running horse before dropping it over the pony. Dan'l earned cheers of respect when he decided to hang the loop from one end of a long pole, vastly extending the mustanger's reach.

"Hell," he quipped to Snowshoe, "someday, hoss, men will get good enough to just throw the ropes."

"Boone," his friend replied, shaking his head, "your foolishness is a caution to screech owls!"

But even Dan'l's clever invention couldn't eliminate the tail-jarring ride on the "hurricane deck" of these Spanish ponies. After picking himself up out of the dirt over and over, Snowshoe roundly cursed all of Creation. Then he shouted out, "Needed: Fools to trail mustangs with Dan'l goddamn Boone! Orphans preferred!"

The first step was choking the horse down to take the fight out of it. Once its feet were tied, the choking lariat was slacked. The horse would rise, trembling and helpless. At this point the Indians turned gentle, approaching each animal and breathing into its nostrils to establish a bond.

Then the horses were blindfolded and saddled with a light breaking saddle. The rider was tied down at the knees. When the blindfold was removed, and its feet untied, the horse inevitably started pitching. Then came a long run. When this run was over, the animal was broken to leather.

Once thus broken, the horses were held outside

the pen by necking them together in pairs so they couldn't run. Gradually, the number of tamed horses was larger than the green mustangs inside the pen.

At the end of the third long, dusty day, even crusty old Snowshoe was elated.

"Plank down your gold, pilgrims!" he roared out. "Fine horseflesh for sale!"

"You're working ahead of the roundup," Dan'l warned him. "We ain't even got a trail to follow, so don't spend no earnings until we make 'em."

Snowshoe scoffed at this. "Boone, I know you. If the price is handsome, you'll drive a herd straight through Hell and deliver it to the devil himself!"

Despite such brave and optimistic joshing, however, Dan'l felt a hard little canker of frustration. All this hard work at the breaking pen had kept him from riding out to hunt down those two renegades. It wasn't Dan'l's way to let trouble fester.

Both men watched the Indians at work. Dan'l hoped they were as good at driving horses as they were at gentling them—all four had hired on for the uncertain drive east.

"Think we can pull stakes tomorrow?" Snowshoe asked.

Dan'l nodded. "We best hurry it up. The herd's wantin' to cut fresh grass."

Their own mounts, too, now required graze. Dan'l and Snowshoe had fed them the last of the corn in their saddle pockets.

"Then again," Snowshoe remarked slyly, tugging at his braided beard, "mayhap us two should go on a little hunt first. A Injin hunt."

Dan'l mulled this. "It's temptin'," he admitted. "But what if they've pulled foot outta these parts by now? We could burn up two, three days tryin' to cut sign on a cold trail."

While the two men spoke, the oldest of the three Papagos, Guadalupe, began walking toward them, slapping his hat against his leg. *Needs more resin for his gloves*, Dan'l thought, reaching for it in his saddle.

"Reckon you're right," Snowshoe conceded. "They might be gone at that. Been quiet around here lately. Mebbe Stratton didn't sweeten the pot enough for 'em 'ere savages—not when they seen what a rough piece of work it is to kill rat bastards like me and you!"

Snowshoe's boast was still ringing in the air as Guadalupe stopped directly in front of Dan'l.

"Señor Boone," he said. "One of the mares, she is foaling now. Should we—"

The sentence literally died in Guadalupe's throat. For at that moment, an arrow punched through the back of his neck and dropped out the front, ripping his vocal cords with it.

"God's garters!" Snowshoe exclaimed when a spurt of warm blood arched into Dan'l's surprised eyes. Guadalupe dropped like a sack of grain, drowning in his own blood. He died, emitting horrible noises like a clogged drain, even as the shocked white men knelt to help him.

"Damnit, that's it!" Dan'l sleeved the blood out of his face. "Snowshoe, tend to your battle gear. And cut out a fresh remount. Before this herd goes anywhere, you and me got a couple boils to lance."

Chapter Nine

The second meeting between Hugh Gilpin, Widow Maker, and River of Blood took place where the first one had: in the hill and arroyo country south of the Nueces River. This terrain offered plenty of hiding places, yet also afforded a good view in all directions.

"Sadly for us, Boone is far too experienced at staying covered," River of Blood explained to Gilpin. "He refuses to dwell in open spaces at rest, and he never sits down unless his back is to a tree. I could not hold a bead on him.

"But this Papago I killed? *He* was the price of Widow Maker's dead war pony. At least that score is avenged."

" 'At least,' " Gilpin repeated, his voice bitter with scorn. "Never mind these foolish contests!

You are supposed to kill Boone, not his hirelings."

"Why don't *you* kill him, white-eyes?" Widow Maker demanded.

Gilpin's thin lips pressed into a tight, annoyed frown. But he understood the point and couldn't dispute it: Killing Boone was much easier said than done. Just consider what Boone did in tackling Widow Maker's horse—such skill was not unheard of among the best red men. But it was always considered an act of desperation, seldom successful. Yet, Boone had succeeded.

Boone . . . confidence was etched deep into that man's insolent features, damn him! *You can bleed me, little men,* Boone's mocking eyes taunted. *But you'll never best me.*

"Never mind," snapped the former revenue collector turned Indian agent. "Just know this: A well-bred dog hunts by nature. Boone will come after *you* now, River of Blood. No doubt he's on your trail even as we speak."

The young Kiowa looked startled. "Have you eaten peyote? He has no cause against me for vengeance. I did not harm him or his blood."

Gilpin shook his head. His wig and three-corner hat were yellow with dust. "It's Boone's foolish code. Chances are, he hardly knew that Papago you killed. But the man was on Boone's payroll. That gives Boone—as he sees it—a certain obligation. So the truth is, you have no choice at this point. *Entiendes?* Understand? My friend, between you and Boone it is now kill or be killed."

This comment was awkward, and River of Blood avoided Widow Maker's eyes. For in truth, it had been "kill or be killed" all along, at least for River of Blood. After all, nothing but warrior pride kept Widow Maker from giving all this up as the bad job it was.

But River of Blood had impetuously sworn on his honor as a Kaitsenko, a Kiowa warrior elite. Now he was bound by *his* code, as surely as Boone was by his: Either he killed Boone, or he must fall on his own knife. Otherwise, his fellow Kaitsenkos would dress him as a woman for the rest of his life.

Gilpin had observed Indians closely for years. He could see how these two were subdued, less boastful; their motivation to kill Boone needed a boost.

"My chief back east," he announced, "offers these as a goodwill gesture—and a reminder that your trade goods are still safe at Nacogdoches."

Gilpin carried a leather musette bag over one shoulder. He opened the flap and removed two fine cast-iron hunting daggers, their blades ornamentally etched. Blood grooves were carved in the blades. He handed one to each surprised Indian.

"These are to remind you," Gilpin repeated, "of the fine quality of the goods awaiting you when you deliver Boone's head. But do not forget that you have other good reasons to kill Boone. Tell me—have you heard about this *Ley Caballo* or Horse Law passed by New Spain?"

Both Indians nodded, their dark eyes flashing pure hatred.

"This law forbids red men from riding horses," Widow Maker replied defiantly. And indeed, many felt it was Spain's biggest mistake in this vast country of proud *indio* horsemen. On the frontier, even a poor man who owned a horse had a completely different status from the "walking poor."

"Well, Boone is no different from the Spanish devils. He, too, supports such laws," Gilpin lied, inspired on the spot to this tactic. "He allows his Indian helpers to ride now, yes. But only because they are stealing *your* horses for him."

The two braves exchanged glances.

"Pochos," River of Blood said with contempt, spitting out the word. It was what Mexicans from the interior called these foreign intruders in the Southwest country.

Gilpin nodded, satisfied. "I must return east soon, to the river you call Great Waters. From here, riding hard, it will be at least twelve sleeps before I arrive. My chief knows you are good men. But in case you fall, he and I must prepare another plan to stop Boone."

Both Indians were still admiring the expensive, well-made daggers. Such fine weapons as white war lords carried!

"We *can* stop him," River of Blood said confidently.

Gilpin said, "I agree. Before we three struck terms, I inquired for miles around. Everyone assured me you two were unmatched at killing. So *let* Boone come for you! You two know this country, he does not. Just keep an eye to the main chance, and Boone's luck *has* to finally play out."

*   *   *

Dan'l and Snowshoe remained back at camp only long enough to lay the dead Papago to rest.

Guadalupe was a "praying Indian," Christianized by Jesuits. So he was buried, along with his meager possessions, in a grave overlooking the river. Dan'l spoke the Lord's Prayer over him. Then he scattered gunpowder over the grave and set it ablaze—the stink would keep predators away.

Immediately afterward, Dan'l and Snowshoe hit the trail in search of Guadalupe's killer. Dan'l left Grayeyes, Buffalo Runner, and Coyote Man in charge of the herd.

"What if them blanket asses steal the herd?" Snowshoe demanded.

Dan'l shrugged. "Ain't nothin' I hate worse, hoss, than seeing another man plow with my heifer. But what choice we got?"

Since graze was getting critically short, Dan'l ordered the Indians to make huge travois. These were to be used to haul chopped sotol roots back to feed the mustangs. It was poor fodder, but better than none. It would have to do until they could shove on.

The two experienced trackers had no trouble finding sign where the Indian ponies had fled from the nearby ridge, bearing southwest. But the serpentine trail took enough turns to make a cow cross-eyed. It twisted and looped through desolate, completely new terrain, where an ambush lurked behind every mesa or fold in the ground.

They crossed a vast region of open, rolling

grassland—grass so high it polished their boots in the stirrups. Then they descended again into dusty sagebrush flats. Dan'l preferred the latter country, for you could see the rattlesnakes better.

"Unusual spring," Dan'l remarked sarcastically, slapping his hat on his thigh. "We've only had two inches of dust."

But swirling, choking clouds of dust weren't their only problem. There were few fixed reference points in this vast openness. At night, Dan'l scratched arrows in the dirt, pointing toward the North Star, so they could head out before the sun rose to give them bearings.

They burned "prairie coal"—dried buffalo dung—for heat, and gnawed on the last of their jerked meat. In the higher elevations they got lucky, shooting and dressing out a pronghorn buck. The meat was tough. But Dan'l rated it higher than Snowshoe's damned jackrabbit stew.

Onward, ever onward they pushed, relentlessly dogging those renegade killers. They found sign, south of the Nueces, where the two Indians met with a third man—a man riding a shod horse. A big, heavy, seventeen-hand horse, judging from the size and depth of the prints.

"That'll be Hugh Gilpin," Dan'l surmised. "Stratton's favorite dirt worker. A perfumed and powdered skunk that robs the widows-and-orphans' poor box and calls it revenue. I figured he'd be in the mix."

Both weary trackers looked out across the vast, arid, yellow-brown expanse ahead of them. Snowshoe, his neatly braided beard now scraggly with neglect, loosed a sigh.

"*Damn* your persuasive tongue, Dan'l Boone! Gaw! This coon rues the day he ever listened to your hogwash. What I'd give to be back at Taos, drunk as Davy's saw!"

This complaint pried open a floodgate. For the next two minutes, while Dan'l's penetrating gaze scoured the country, Snowshoe went at it. He shouted and cursed and sprayed spittle and shook his fist at all Creation.

When his friend finally finished his litany of woes, Dan'l said calmly, "You strain at gnats while you swallow camels."

"Goddamnit, Boone! You always spout Scripture, but I ain't no preacher. Spell that out plain."

"It means you best quitcher bellyaching and tend to your job, mister! That plain enough?"

Dan'l nudged his lineback dun into weary motion again. "It means you stow all the noise and keep a weather eye out. We got Innuns to kill, but you best pray we spot them first. This is their range, old son, not ourn. That sorter makes us the prey, not the hunters."

Chapter Ten

Time was growing critical now, so Dan'l and Snowshoe decided to enlist Indian taboo on their side.

They took to holing up by day and stalking by night. Very few Indians ventured outside the firelight after sunset, fearing they lost their protective medicine when the sun went down. Just as important—many lost their will to fight. It was the same way with painting their faces. Dan'l had seen strong, brave warriors flee from an easy victory if they could not paint and dance first.

"These sneaking sons-a-bitches haven't faced us once in a fair fight," Dan'l announced with grim determination. "They tried to burn us to ashes in our sleep. The Comanche wounded me from ambush first before he had the oysters to attack. And they killed Guadalupe from ambush, too. Never gave him a fighting chance, but they'll add a notch to their coup sticks.

"So never mind any 'fair fight' from here on out, Snowshoe. We got two snakes to stomp on is all, y'unnerstan'? Let's crush 'em, then point our bridles to home."

Sign was not always easy to find in the moonlight, especially across the windswept flats. The men tracked north from the Nueces, bearing toward the old Spanish mission—long abandoned—at Carrizo Springs. Twice Dan'l found horse droppings, fresher each time.

"We're closing in on 'em," Dan'l added, silently debating something. "But directly, the sun will up. Course, that don't mean they'll be up right with it. Most Indians are damned late sleepers."

"Not always," Snowshoe reminded him. " 'Member how them Senecas, up in the Hudson Country, drunk plenty o' water on the night before they attacked us right at sunup? Achin' bladders rolled 'em out early."

"You see *plenty* of water anywhere near here, hoss? Anyhow, nuff chinwag about it. We'll push on ahead till sunrise. Happens we find 'em asleep, that's where they'll rot. It'll be mercy compared to what they deserve. But seeing as how it was Lansford Stratton and Hugh Gilpin who prodded 'em, I don't begrudge a little mercy."

"Forgive your enemies," Snowshoe agreed piously. "After you hang the bastards."

The two friends shoved on, eating grit, the only sound the mournful singing of the wind and the chinking of bit rings. Their trail wound through a series of small redrock canyons.

Abruptly, rising up from a cutbank at the end of a narrow canyon, Dan'l raised one hand to warn his friend. Snowshoe nudged his mule up beside Dan'l.

"What's on the spit, Sheltowee?" he whispered.

Dan'l pointed ahead in the grainy, blue-black light. "Up yonder," he whispered. " 'Bout a hunnert yards—see it?"

Snowshoe squinted, trying to read the inky fathoms. "Shaw! Boone, you're either loco or a goldang cat. Boy, this child don't see nothin' but dark."

"You will. Hobble your mule," Dan'l told him, swinging down himself. "From here it's shank's mare."

They drew in closer, leapfrogging between boulders and squat palo duro trees. Finally even Snowshoe spotted them: two low windbreaks made of stones and boughs. And behind each, a low, blanket-covered mound exactly the size and shape of a man.

"God's garters!" Snowshoe gloated in a whisper. "Two buzzards dozin' on a fence. Let's plink 'em, Dan'l."

But Dan'l stayed his friend with a grip like an eagle's talon. "Hang fire, Jeddiah. Could be a false camp. Where's their horses?"

As if to answer that very question, a snorting whinny sounded from below and to their left.

"Hid in that arroyo yonder," Snowshoe replied

triumphantly. *"That's* where. Let's do for 'em, Dan'l."

Something still felt wrong to Dan'l—little pin-prickles of warning numbed his skull. He sensed more danger than he could account for from the signs. But he was tired, trail-worn, weary, and hungry. Maybe all that, he reasoned, had skewed his judgment—made him "skeery," as the hillmen called being overly cautious.

"All right. Check your loads first," he whispered. "Morning dew might've clumped our powder."

They squatted on their ankles to inspect their pistols and long-irons, making sure the primer and main charges were dry. Then, moving cat-footed, they continued forward quietly. Snowshoe listed badly on his carved foot, but made remarkably good time with little noise.

Dan'l knew first-hand that lead balls did extraordinary damage to a human body. But he also knew there was only one shot that guaranteed a kill with one bullet: a shot directly into the brain. He recalled once shooting a Mohawk plumb through the heart, yet the man still got off a good toss with his tomahawk before he expired.

So both men moved dangerously close: within spitting range. Dan'l eased his pistol's trigger back from half-to full-cock. His index finger slipped inside the trigger-guard and wrapped the trigger.

Don't Injuns snore? Dan'l wondered. These were silent sleepers, though it was true the steady wind might be masking their breathing noises. Willing himself steady, Dan'l started to draw a bead on the Indian nearest the fire.

Then, in just an eyeblink's time, his heart turned over as Dan'l realized how they'd been duped. Like two greenhorns, he and Snowshoe had fallen for the old ruse of a false camp. For Dan'l could see clearly now that the 'head' wrapped in that blanket was in fact a rock—and the rest of the 'man' was dirt and stones.

"Mira!" said a scornful voice behind them in Spanish. "Look! The mighty white legends!"

At the sound, both men bucked as if they'd been butt-shot. Dan'l heard Snowshoe cry out when an arrow punched into him from behind, dropping the big man in his tracks.

But Dan'l's honed reflexes saved him. Even as he bucked, he moved a hair faster than his friend. Dan'l fell hard to his right and rolled over onto his back, sitting up fast with his short gun at the ready.

The day's new light gave Dan'l just enough time to recognize the ugly Comanche who had attacked him near the holding pen. Dan'l fired his lower barrel, missed, cursed; he rolled hard to the right, barely avoiding a flurry of arrows from the Comanche's bow. Dan'l managed to snap the upper barrel into place.

With no time to aim, he only pointed and fired. His shot shattered the Comanche's right rib cage and tore into lung tissue, not killing him but knocking him out of the fight. The big Kiowa who had tagged Snowshoe raised a battle-ax to throw at Dan'l.

His long gun was out of reach. With only a second to react, Dan'l raised his right foot and snatched the knife out of his boot.

His throw was a bit rushed, his aim a bit off, and on top of that it was a skinning knife with a curved blade. But Dan'l managed to cut a neat slice off the inside of the Kiowa's upraised arm. He grunted in pain, dropped his weapon, and fled toward his hidden horse.

Dan'l snatched up Patsy and got a snap shot off, missing in the grayish gloom of dawn. Once he was sure the Kiowa had actually fled, Dan'l finished the Comanche off with his own knife. So much for Indian superstition about fear of the dark, Dan'l berated himself.

Then he turned to see if Snowshoe still belonged to the living.

About four hundred miles due east of Carrizo Springs, along the west bank of the Mississippi River, things were starting to look mighty lively around the normally sleepy settlement of French-man's Lick.

The place was too rustic to describe it as even a village. Besides the ferry landing, there was just a tumbledown mill with a crude aqueduct, a sprawling livery barn, and a two-room tavern with a blacksmith's forge attached by a dogtrot. But presently, the area boasted far more folks than it usually saw in two months.

One of them was Lansford Stratton. Publicly, he made much stirring and to-do about "touring New Spain's northern outposts to personally study the condition of horsemanship there." But secretly, he had arrived to discreetly oversee the possible military operation against Boone. Toward that end, the bulk of Lev Vogel's private army was secretly camped on the east bank of the river.

But Stratton was unpleasantly surprised to learn that others, too, were showing up. For Dame Rumor had long been spreading the boast Daniel Boone made many months ago: that he would be coming to the Lick, driving the fabled Western mustangs before him.

One of those who showed up, his curiosity piqued, was Abbot Fontaine, one of the river region's most well-known horse traders. An open enemy of Britain, and a stout supporter of Boone and his "mountain rabble," it wasn't long before Fontaine and Stratton locked horns at the local tavern.

"The equestrian future of this *British colony*," Stratton repeated, "belongs to big chestnuts and bays bred from Arabians and Barbs. Solid colors, long legs, pure breeds."

Fontaine drained a pewter tankard of ale and banged it onto the counter. Then he removed his hat and whacked at flies with it. He had long silver hair and a face like a hatchet.

"I've seen your horses, Guv'nor. They're big, all right, and they're pretty. But the cowl does not make the monk! I've yet to see Daniel Boone on a *pretty* horse. But I'll wager we will see Squire's boy soon. For he's about to introduce—for *breeding* purposes, mind you, m'lord—a superior new line of Western horses."

It was Lev Vogel, seated beside Stratton at a crude deal table, who laughed first.

"Ha!" the Russian snorted. "Boone's cake is dough, friend." He started to add something else, but Stratton looked a warning at him.

"You're talking through the back of your neck," Stratton assured the trader. "Only look at the situation here in Civilization. *We* have roads. Yet one good rain turns them to impassable hog wallows. I grant that Boone may indeed *catch* some of these worthless scrub ponies. But he has no trail to follow across land totally bereft of water. My best military advisors assure me it cannot be done."

"Well, strike a light! Someone forgot to tell Boone. Your 'best advisors' are naught but a misbegotten pack of asses. Daniel Boone will not only bring a herd—but those animals will eventually sink your big breeds, and your fortune with them, Stratton."

Stratton's long, pale face was suddenly splotched with anger. This insolent knave ought to be whipped for his surly words and tone. But Stratton knew he must tread carefully here. He did not want to become the center of attention with a possible massacre looming—there were so-called "people's courts" out here. And Boone was popular with the vulgar masses.

"Sir," Stratton said with false civility, "I'll wager you one hundred pieces of eight that a 'mustang' will never touch the east bank of the Mississippi— not in company with Daniel Boone, at any rate."

The amount gave Fontaine pause: The piece of eight was the Spanish silver dollar, worth eight bits Continental. One hundred dollars, in the latter half of the eighteenth century, could keep a family of ten comfortable for half a year. But finally he nodded.

"If you wish to play ducks and drakes with your money, m'lord, it's no affair of mine. *Done!*"

After Fontaine left, Stratton told Vogel quietly, "I shouldn't be seen with you again. I'm only waiting for Gilpin to arrive with a fuller report. Then I mean to fade."

Vogel scowled. "You talk like combat is imminent. I thought you swore up and down Boone couldn't make it? That he'd either die out West or return without a herd."

"Don't put words in my mouth," Stratton snapped. "A prudent man plans for the worst. I have mirror stations and runners in place as far west as the Sabine River. So I already know that Boone has a herd. But I know nothing of his progress with it. Reports are very sketchy and not always reliable. I need to confer with Gilpin. Meantime, *you* had better tend to your own obligations, Lev."

"Go to hell!" Vogel scowled, his face tightening like a fist. Stratton was referring to the brash saboteur who had nearly caused a riot by draining all his men's rum. If Stratton had not purchased an extra keg from a passing keelboat, Vogel might have been skinned alive by his own men. And that keg wouldn't last forever. Not with the drunken sots Vogel employed.

"It's no fault of mine," Vogel went on, "if Boone is more popular than you care to admit. His allies are obviously everywhere. What is it, Nika?" he added, for his most trusted man had just entered the tavern and approached their table.

Nikolai Bulgakov bent forward and spoke low in his superior's ear. Stratton watched a smile divide Vogel's face.

Vogel looked at Stratton and said, "You recall Armand? The dead man we found?"

"The man with the neat knife slice in his heart?"

Vogel nodded. "As I said, Boone's allies are everywhere. But Nika here tells me he has spotted the one who surely killed Armand. A trap is being laid. And you may be pleasantly surprised when you lay eyes on the beautiful little she-bitch."

Chapter Eleven

"*There's* your damned tea you been whining for," Dan'l said.

Snowshoe had just come to about twenty minutes earlier. He was still too weak—and in too much pain—to accept the bark cup of sassafras tea. Dan'l held it for him while he sipped.

"Tea? Tastes more like cold piss. H'ar now!" Snowshoe fussed. "You're sloppin' it all over my beard, Boone, damn ye!"

At this, Dan'l's weary face creased itself in a wide grin. "Aye, I reckon you'll live after all, for your tongue has come sassy again. I had to leave the arrow point inside you, old hoss. Naught else for it—she sank deep under the muscle."

"I feel it. By God! It's my second one!" Snowshoe boasted. "Makes me a *true* flint-hearted bastard."

Despite the pain contorting his face, Snowshoe added eagerly, "What about that Comanch?"

"Cold as a wagon wheel."

Snowshoe laughed, immediately wincing at the pain under his left shoulder blade. "Good man, Boone. But that Kiowa foxed us, anh?"

Dan'l, now busy cutting bore patches, nodded. "Right from the get-go, them two Injuns've been struttin' and preenin'. But each time we tried to put 'em through their facings, tried to *see* if they're such toughens, they acted like fish in hot weather and headed for the bottom. Well, one's floated up dead. I kallate the other means to sink out of sight again."

"God's truth," Snowshoe replied weakly. "So we'll sink down to his level and hook the sumbitch."

Dan'l ran a patch through the bore of his long gun. "*We* is you and your gran'maw, hoss. *I'm* riding out, and you're staying put right here till you're strong enough to return to the horse pen and make yourself useful. I'll meet you back there."

"Sell your ass, Boone! I kin ride. You don't—"

"Whack the cork, old campaigner. I said you'll stay here," Dan'l repeated, his tone brooking no defiance. "Elsewise, you'll just go puny on me. A man goes puny, he's worthless. It ain't just your being stove up—all this poor diet lately has got both of us down with the squitters, weak as kittens. You'll go puny and die on me. Then I got to bury your worthless carcass."

Dan'l squared his shoulders, stood, whistled for

his dun. "I've got my belly full of these damn delays. We got a herd to push east. Before the next sunset," he vowed, "I mean to have that Kiowa walking with his ancestors."

Sha-hee-ka stroked only enough to stay out in the swift channel of the Mississippi.

Between spurts of paddling, she lay flat in the shallow bateau, making a low profile on the moonlit river. Soon the War Woman drew even with a gravel bar she had recently fixed in memory. She paddled out of the current and headed rapidly toward shore.

Nervous fear made her alert and slightly sweaty in the nighttime humidity. Mosquitoes were relentless here along the wooded coastal plain near the river, new hatches appearing every day. But she had smeared her exposed skin with the dark juice of the berry called citronella, and that kept many of them off.

She dragged the light boat out of the water and hid it in a bracken of ferns. Then, for a long time, she paused to listen.

It had rained earlier, and now it was so quiet she could hear the trees drip. The only other sound was the steady crackle of insects, and that sound always reassured her.

Tonight was to be Sha-hee-ka's boldest move yet against Lev Vogel's cutthroat army. In draining the liquor rations, Sha-hee-ka now realized she had only struck at the branches of Vogel's power; now she meant to destroy the *roots*.

She had finally, after much dangerous scouting,

located Vogel's powder magazine. And tonight she meant to kill the guard and ruin that powder. She didn't have to actually ignite it—only foul it with a bit of damp earth so it would burn unevenly. Even mildly contaminated grains were useless. Black powder would be much harder to replace, around here, than liquor had been. It might take many days, longer if they were late in discovering it. And Daniel might well return during that delay.

Sha-hee-ka knew her plan was far from perfect. Of course, it had been scratched out quickly in the dirt. But she was trained to act, not sit upon the ground and wail about the odds life heaped against her.

And against Daniel. For Sha-hee-ka understood by now the formidable trap Boone might be heading into. She had watched the training lately and knew what these men meant to do.

Advance scouts had crossed the river to watch for first signs of Boone's arrival. At a signal from them, Vogel's men would deploy, in two squads, into the trees directly across from the eastern terminus of the ferry.

The ferry itself would be a giant floating death trap: vulnerable and very, very slow, for it was pulled across by hand on a fixed rope-and-pulley. It was three connected rafts, each thirty feet by forty feet. The men would wait until it was nearly across. Then both squads would charge out of the trees, full-front face, front row kneeling.

One would maintain a steady volley of fire until every man and animal on the helpless rafts was dead or dying; the other would race to the river's edge and fire upon any remaining men or animals waiting on the west bank. The river was fairly narrow here—narrow enough that even those waiting on the opposite shore would suffer casualties before they could flee.

If any mustangs did survive, they would escape. And Sha-hee-ka had heard Stratton himself give emphatic orders that every pony was to be hunted down and slaughtered. Even if Sha-hee-ka did not admire Daniel Boone as much as she did, she could not permit this to happen. While she had breath in her nostrils, she would fight Stratton and Vogel.

But will alone could not get it done. The powder magazine she now had in sight was actually a sturdy, two-wheeled cassion upon which was mounted a reinforced iron box. It was kept upwind of the squad fires, under constant guard.

Crouched down low behind a fallen tree, Sha-hee-ka could see the bored sentry in the silver moonwash. He sat on one of the cassion's iron-reinforced wheels, vacant-eyed and rabbit-toothed. A musketoon—a sawed-off German musket—depended from one shoulder.

Closer, yet closer, feeling each stick underfoot so it would not snap. Now Sha-hee-ka could smell the sentry's rancid-sweat odor.

But what was wrong? Some knowledge more primitive than thought prickled her skin. The Cherokee princess took one more cautious step.

The moment she did, two things happened almost simultaneously. First, Sha-hee-ka realized with a cold shudder exactly what was wrong: *The insect noise had fallen silent.* A heartbeat later, a rawhide loop closed around her ankle, and she was snared like a rabbit.

A bent sapling *whooshed* straight up; Sha-hee-ka was jerked roughly off the ground, her neck twisting painfully. A moment later, she hung upside down, dangling helpless from her ankle loop. Blood rushed into her face and throbbed hard in her ears.

Harsh laughter and cheers erupted from the darkness around her.

"Boone's lickspittles are everywhere," came the eloquent baritone voice of Lansford Stratton out of the night. "Even his half-breed whores. Lev, this woman is timely met! We'll let her live long enough to see her hero cut down like a hog."

A clammy hand suddenly stroked her leg, feeling the shapely muscle, and Sha-hee-ka shivered with revulsion.

"Afterward," Stratton added, much closer now, "to reward your men for a job well done, we'll let them all line up for a turn on this little beauty. Then she can join her hero in the same grave."

"Fine by me," Vogel agreed. "But I'm taking my turn tonight."

Dan'l paused in the lee of a mesa and sleeved sweat off his forehead. His nose was raw with sunburn, but his forehead was still pale from the protection of his wide-brimmed hat.

He checked the sun's position and estimated it was late in the forenoon. Ragged tatters of cirrus cloud drifted across a mother-of-pearl sky. Ahead, wind-scoured alkali flats stretched on between bare rock mesas. To his right, a low ridge of volcanic scree. To his left, hazy desert stretched toward the heart of Old Mexico. And behind, endless expanses of purple sage and the tall cacti known as Spanish Bayonets.

Lord God Almighty, but he was sick of it! A man forgot, until trapped long enough out here, how beautiful Kentucky could be in spring when the silver spruces started to bud.

But he was also sick of this goddamn Kiowa. If Dan'l ignored him, he'd only strike again from hiding and kill again. So now Dan'l meant to ride him down and plant him.

Dan'l cut sign on the Kiowa, lost it on hardpan, picked it up again in a sandy wash near the Mater Dolorosa River. The long hunter's bones ached, his eyes burned, his tongue had begun to swell in his mouth.

When he was so tired he was sliding from his horse, Dan'l finally paused in a cottonwood copse. He staked his dun to the saddle horn, using the saddle as his pillow. After an hour's fitful sleep, he pushed on.

Nature battered him, but Dan'l pressed doggedly forward. He got caught flush in a sudden, straight-down rain shower that left poke marks in the dirt. He rode on, ignoring the hard slapping of the rain, occasionally singing snatches of "Yankee Doodle" to rally himself and his dun.

Something moved in the tail of his eye. Dan'l flicked his eyes to the right and spotted faint dust puffs. Two hard little points of light glittered in Dan'l's gaze.

"Oh, we'll be huggin', John," Dan'l vowed softly, using the name whites on the frontier used to address Indians. He reined in the direction of the puffs.

By now the lineback was as beat-out as Dan'l. But this was a long, descending slope. Dan'l knew a gallop or hard run, even downhill, could ruin a winded horse. So he opted for a lively trot—a tired horse would rebel during a run, but would trot until it dropped.

Within three or four miles, by Dan'l's reckoning, his hunch turned to a certainty: He recognized the Kiowa's little buckskin. It took the renegade some time to notice his pursuer. When he did, he lashed his pony to a gallop with a light sisal whip he carried in his sash.

Dan'l felt his exhaustion ebb, felt the hunting instinct begin to thrum in his blood.

"By God, you can ride to China, feather-head," Dan'l vowed through clenched teeth. "You still got an appointment with Patsy gal."

Dan'l resisted the urge to push his dun faster. He gambled on the buckskin's being tired, too, and the gamble paid off. After a few minutes, the little Indian cayuse began to falter.

Dan'l held his dun to a trot and saw that he was gaining. The big Kiowa, however, was as agile on horseback as his dead companion had been— while Dan'l closed in, he spun around and launched a flurry of arrows.

Dan'l hunched small as the deadly projectiles

sliced past. One stuck in his saddle fender, another tore through his buckskin shirt with a hard tug that pulled the shirt halfway around on him. Dan'l hated to waste a bullet at this range. But the Kiowa was preparing to launch another fistful of arrows. Dan'l swung Patsy up into his shoulder and snapped off a round.

"Well, I'm a Dutchman!"

Dan'l grinned ear to ear when the Kiowa's osage-wood bow suddenly snapped like a wishbone. "Couldn't do that again even if I aimed!"

Dan'l poked Patsy into her saddle boot and eased his pistol out of the holster. By now the game little buckskin was blowing bloody foam. Still it pressed on, the warrior driving it mercilessly.

Dan'l had two primed loads waiting, both in his short-gun. He was close enough now to shoot the horse, but figured he was about to run it dead anyway. Might's well save the round, he decided. That Kiowa wasn't about to sell his soul cheaply.

That thought still echoed when the warrior twisted round in the saddle and hurled a stone-headed hatchet dead-center at Dan'l.

It twirled straight at Dan'l's chest. Reacting instantly, Dan'l flexed his left arm and twisted half-right, all he had time to do. He took the hit on the powerful, bunched muscle of his shoulder. Luckily, the sharpened edge didn't strike, but the haft. Still, an impact like a mule kick punched his arm. It went numb like a 'funny bone,' but didn't feel so damn funny, Dan'l groused to himself.

A second later, Dan'l roared out a curse: At the

shock of impact, he'd also lost his grip on his pistol. It went bouncing and rolling behind him, and now Dan'l had only one hope: Ride that Kiowa down.

"Hi-ya! Hii-*ya*!" Dan'l urged the lineback to a run now. Within a few minutes, he was almost close enough to touch his enemy's horse on the rump.

The resourceful Kiowa had been driving his buckskin on with a sisal whip. But now he threw it down and reached into a saddle pocket. Dan'l saw his right hand emerge gripping a long "blacksnake" whip with a knotted popper. The Kaintuck soon discovered that savage was no novice with it, either.

Fwap! Fwap, fwap!

The second snapping pop ripped Dan'l's right cheek open, the third tore his hat off. More blows opened a cut over his eye and made his skull ring. Blow after well-aimed blow lacerated Dan'l's neck and hands.

Fwap! Fwap, fwap!

This Kiowa was whaling the tar out of him, and Dan'l felt hot rage fill him as if he were a bucket under a tap. His right hand was still plenty tender from that Comanche arrow that had drilled it. Yet, somehow, Dan'l managed to grab hold of the flailing popper. Roaring like a sore-tailed bear, Dan'l flexed his muscles and pulled hard.

With a shrill yip of surprise, the Kiowa was ripped out of his saddle before he could let go. He flew back over his pony's rump, crashed to the ground hard, rolled once—and then Dan'l's line-back was on him!

By instinct, for tame horses avoided stepping on people, the lineback made a magnificent effort to avoid this human obstacle. But it was too sudden. Both front feet landed square on the Indian's chest, crushing it like an eggshell.

Dan'l waited until the Indian had chanted his death-song through blood-frothed lips. Then he showed mercy and sliced his throat quick and clean.

Grim-faced, sweat streaking the dirt, his chest heaving hard from the exertion, Dan'l watched his enemy finally give up the ghost. His heels scratched at the dirt briefly, and then he was still as stone.

"Safe on the reservation at last," Dan'l told the dead man at his feet. "You were a back-shooter, and good thing for you I'm a Christian, or you'da died slow, John."

Dan'l turned and whistled for his dun.

"Now, by God," Dan'l announced to the world as he swung up into leather, "we can finally get down to work."

Dan'l reined round in a tight circle, then abruptly drew up short, gaping in slack-jawed astonishment. For there, perhaps two hundred yards over on the next ridge, a magnificent white mustang paced with dream-like smoothness.

The Pacer . . . Dan'l watched his flowing mane and tail ripple like guidons in the wind. And then the vision—if that's what it was, perhaps spawned by nerves and exhaustion—was over.

"Second time I've seen you," Dan'l whispered. "I thankee for the warning."

He was ready. For as bad as things had been, this vision promised that the worst was yet to come.

Chapter Twelve

With Widow Maker and River of Blood finally sent under, Daniel Boone began the first trail drive of his life.

Never mind, Dan'l told the rest, that there was no trail yet. Boone figured there'd damn sure be one after they blazed it. And never mind, too, that some Philadelphia lawyer in a wig and velvet doublet would figure out a way to charge tolls on it. Dan'l had learned long ago that for every bold man willing to take a risk, there were five cowards waiting to profit from it. Indeed, he feared that fact would someday become a strong nation's epitaph.

But "someday" was a long way off! For now, Dan'l struggled from hour to hour, too dog-tired to think about anything but the awesome task at hand.

Neither Dan'l, Snowshoe, nor their three Indian herders were always sure exactly who was in charge—the men or these damned notional horses. They were saddle-broken—just barely— but hardly docile.

Dan'l had learned, over the years, that horses were nothing like cattle when being herded. They followed the commands of their master stallions, not the goadings of men.

Thus, a *manada* of horses, unlike a herd of cows, was always on the verge of losing its group cohesion. True, cows stampeded at the sound of a cough or a mutter of thunder; but they ran together, as a unit. Horses bolted individually. And at night, horses refused to lie down and sleep together on a bedground. Most slept on their feet; Dan'l rarely saw them lay down except to roll.

When Dan'l sensed that the band was especially restless, he sought out hardpan and pushed Poco Loco hard. Tender-footed horses were less likely to bolt. But some of the mares, fillies, and colts grew too lame and slowed their progress.

Dan'l had anticipated this problem. He had the Indians quickly cut crude horseshoes from pieces of rawhide. Dan'l used shingling nails to attach them. They provided great relief to the horse, which also built more trust between animals and men.

"By God, Dan boy," Snowshoe muttered, riding up beside his friend. It was late on the second morning after the push had begun, and Snowshoe was getting full movement back after his wounding. "That cussed Apache," Snowshoe went on, "has got his sights on Malachi! He means to eat my mule, that red heathen. You seen how he's doin'?"

Dan'l hid a smile behind his hand. In fact, Grayeyes was only joshing the redbeard. But Snowshoe had sidekicked with that flea-bitten old mule for years now and loved Malachi like a blood brother. He saw no humor in the Apache's jokes. Now, seeing the two whiteskins watching him, Grayeyes nudged his cayuse close to them for a moment.

The Apache reached out and pinched Malachi's generous roll of neck fat. The mule nervously sidehopped away.

"Mmm! Damn good fixens, uh?" he said in loud English.

"H'ar now!" It gave Snowshoe fits every time the Indian touched his mule. "Don't hem that ani-mule, you pagan gut-eater! Mister, you didn't jist *touch* no white buffalo, you et the damn thing!"

Dan'l laughed so hard he had to pretend he was hawking up phlegm. Grayeyes rode back to his herding duties, slyly grinning. Snowshoe, already cantankerous from tobacco starvation, cussed a blue streak. He even made up some curses Dan'l had never heard.

"All that hot-jawin'," Dan'l rebuked him, "and today is the Sabbath! You ain't even said good morning to Jesus yet."

Snowshoe looked up at the sky. "Good morning, Lord, how's by you and your Pa? Now *will* you two fellas please damn Boone right straight to Hell?"

"Hell don't want me," Dan'l scoffed. "They're afraid I'd take over and find a route outta there.

Now quitcher bitchen and stir your stump. Go help them 'Pagos turn that east flank. They're about to run into gopher holes."

Despite this ongoing tension between Snowshoe and the Indians, all three red men remained friendly toward him. All of them had nodded when Dan'l explained that Snowshoe had no squaw. Bachelors were not welcome in Puritan America, where they were watched with suspicion, fined, even assessed the "bachelor tax." It was little different for unmarried Indians. Many deserted their tribes, as these herders had done, and became independent *hombres de campo*, men of the wilderness.

Dan'l didn't care a jackstraw for all that. He figured every damn one of them was sure-god earning their breakfast this trip. This drive was almost four hundred miles, much of it across parched and burning ground that Dan'l didn't know well. Forage and water became the twin horns of an unrelenting dilemma.

More than once, Malachi's uncanny ability to sniff water saved them. But even relief brought new disasters. Near the few watering holes, Dan'l's crew was forced to keep big brush fires going at night so mosquitoes and flies wouldn't make the herd frantic. Dan'l had once seen horses near Santa Fe go so fly-mad they had to be killed.

Hot nights set in, and night heat was always more suffocating. At the end of the first week of the drive, they made camp against a rise of ground for wind shelter. This was near the Pecos River, and there was lush grass as well as good shade.

"We'll lay over for two days," Dan'l announced. "Let the herd rest and graze a mite. God knows what's ahead."

"Aye, we better," Snowshoe agreed. "But you seen them wolf tracks back yonder? We're edging into panther and wolf country."

Dan'l nodded. His eyes, slitted against the sun, watched the lead stallion carefully.

"Poco Loco smells 'em," Dan'l said. "Panthers especially. You can see he's been clawed onct already, see all them scars on his back? Panthers like to drop outta trees onto a horse's back. I seen Poco Loco get skittish, while back, and lead the herd from out front."

Snowshoe, busy digging at ticks in his beard braids, frowned at this. He took Dan'l's meaning—it was a dangerous sign. When a master stallion led from out front, rather than from behind, the band was in trouble. A front runner could not discipline the stragglers; nor could he be trusted not to bolt if there was bad trouble, deserting the rest when he was most needed.

The Papago twin named Buffalo Runner conferred with Grayeyes in Spanish. The Apache turned to Dan'l.

"Best way keep stallion calm," he said in English, "you rub his nose in puma blood. For true, it work."

Puma was the local word for panther. Dan'l gazed toward the surrounding pine ridges. Then he gauged the generous moonlight.

"Panthers hunt by night," he said. "Reckon I'll see can I shoot one."

Snowshoe made a rude sound with his lips. "Them Indian legends're bunk. You—"

"I was thinking out loud," Dan'l cut him off. "Not asking for your advice."

Two hours later Dan'l returned to camp with a dead panther—but dragging it by a long rope, for even his well-disciplined lineback dun refused to carry the hated predator on its back.

Dan'l kept it well downwind of the herd and led Poco Loco to the carcass, blindfolding him first. The stallion squealed and began pawing, kicking, and biting the carcass. When he calmed, Dan'l smeared puma blood on Poco Loco's nose.

"We wore off the panic edge," a weary Dan'l told Snowshoe. "He *should* stand and fight, happens panthers attack now."

It was late by now, the wee hours when the yellow moon begins to turn a ghostly white. Bats flitted overhead, shadowy and furtive, communicating in squeals. The herd was gathered nearby in a grassy meadow, some grazing, some asleep on their feet. The Indians slept like spokes around the hub of a still-glowing firepit, built for smoke, not heat.

Malachi, tethered nearby, brayed pitifully. The love-struck mule was pining to be near his favorite mare. Normally, Dan'l knew, Snowshoe would let him go, for stallions tolerated mules well. But now Snowshoe refused to let him out of his sight, for fear Grayeyes might roast him.

"If it ain't pumas," Snowshoe groused, having trouble sleeping in this prickly heat, "then it's renegade killers. If it ain't Espanish soldiers, it's killer

118

dust storms. When it ain't drought, why then it's gully-washers! But by God, Dan boy, leastways we don't let no man tax the goldang meat we eat! This child don't *want* no damned civ'lization. Gaw! I call it syphilization."

" 'It's the empty spaces that will save us,' " Dan'l agreed, quoting one of Squire Boone's favorite sayings.

Dan'l paused, recalling how he had spotted the omen of the Pacing White Mustang a second time. He had said nothing to Snowshoe about this sighting. But it was the Pacer Dan'l had in mind when he added, just before he dozed off, "Course, them spaces ain't never actually empty, are they?"

Dan'l soon discovered that they had prepared well—but for the wrong disaster.

It seemed to him that he had just tumbled over the threshold into sleep. Suddenly the Indians jolted him out of his dreams with their shouted cry: *"Lobos!"*

Wolves! Dan'l saw the whole nightmare scene the moment he sat up, already reaching for his long-gun.

A slavering pack of shaggy gray timber wolves— perhaps a score of them—had isolated a few mares and colts from the main gather. The main band did not run. Rather, by instinct they formed a circle, heads out, colts in the center.

They were safe in their numbers. However, the isolated horses were in serious danger. The snarling, darting wolves went directly for the hindquarters, trying to hamstring their quarry. Dan'l watched a pair of them leap into action at the same moment, cleverly working one horse: One clung to the mustang's throat, the other went for the hind sinews.

Dan'l could not fire from this distance without hitting a horse. Snowshoe blasted a round into the air, but the starving wolves paid it no heed. All five men raced toward the snarling, whinnying confusion.

Dan'l saw that the beleaguered mustangs were not defenseless. One frenzied mare, protecting her colt, seized an overbold wolf by the back, flipped it into the air, then stomped it repeatedly with her front feet. But the main gather would not rush to the defense—wolf attacks, Dan'l recalled, paralyzed most horses the way fires did.

Now the Indians sent arrows humming into the wolf pack. Dan'l watched Snowshoe, too, clear a bead line and send a lead ball punching into a lobo. Dan'l was about to drop one himself when Grayeyes's voice roared out: "Boone! *Cuidado! Mira detrás!*"

But the warning to look behind him came too late. Dan'l felt something slam into his legs, bowling him over. The moment he was down, at least a half dozen snarling timber wolves leapt to the feast.

Teeth slashed through his buckskin trousers, ripped into skin; but Dan'l knew he'd never walk again if that wolf managed to sever the tendons behind his knees.

Dan'l roared, twisted half-about, fired his long-gun point-blank. The wolf's salivating maw disappeared in a spray of smashed fangs and broken jawbone.

But quick as a finger snap, another wolf was on him, fighting to gain purchase on his throat. And yet another, this one attacking his knee tendons.

Dan'l rolled hard, flailing and kicking, cursing blue murder while he clawed out his short-gun. He could whiff the shaggy, musty stink of the beasts. His pistol bucked in his fist, and the .38 caliber ball caught one wolf in the belly. A second later, a Papago arrow sent the other wolf howling off into the darkness.

Dan'l was on his feet again, sassy as a jaybird, recharging Patsy. He felt blood dripping down his legs, but Dan'l knew from experience the bites were not deep. Two of the colts, however, were not so fortunate. One was already half-gutted, the other still twitching in death convulsions as several wolves ripped its entrails out.

When a few more wolves had been killed, the rest finally fled, many carrying bloody meat in their mouths.

"Next time," Snowshoe complained, putting a bullet in a screaming mare, "it'll be panthers!"

"There'll be something," Dan'l agreed, doing a quick head count of the Indians and pack animals. "One damned thing after another. Always is. But never mind. We'd best drive the *manada* a few miles farther on. They won't settle down near their dead. Since even Grayeyes can't eat all that horsemeat, and I ain't in no mood to bury it, that means we pull up stakes now."

Snowshoe, dog-tired, shook a ham-sized fist at

the star-shot sky. " 'Let there be jackasses and fools and half-wits!' our Lord declared. 'Let there be men who breathe risks like air, who labor like galley slaves and profit like chimney sweeps!' And yea, verily, *The mustangers were born!*"

Chapter Thirteen

Later in the coming century, when Dan'l's name and pioneering exploits had already passed into American legend, men would rightly begin to celebrate the new "cowboys." But in truth, the American West first created many fine "horseboys." Eventually, these men would drive more than a million wild mustangs off their free ranges and into corrals. Without their risks and hard work, the mounted cowboys on their superb little "cow ponies" could never have emerged.

But distant glory was only today's sweat and muscle and backbreaking labor. And trouble, cussed *trouble*, thought Dan'l.

The new year, out West, had started with a January chinook—a warming wind from the southwest that usually meant bad weather. And sure enough, it came. From too little water, the beleaguered mustangers and their herd crossed into the tall-grass prairie east of the 100th meridian—where torrential rains began to plague them.

The mustangers donned slickers and kept their lariats well greased with bear fat. Otherwise, they'd go water-limp, then stiffen when they dried. Men and animals tucked their heads down and slogged on, keeping to high ground when possible.

Then, inexplicably, the rain just stopped, as suddenly as a door slamming shut. They again pushed through a long stretch of barren, grassless sand hills. Before long, Dan'l noticed "the creeps" had begun to plague some of the herd—a generally weakened condition brought on by scant diet.

"Happens we don't hit grass right damn quick," Dan'l muttered on their fourth day through poor graze, "these horses're buzzard bait. They're looking poorly."

Snowshoe had to concur, for both men had already witnessed the progress of the creeps in cattle back east. First the animals thinned down to skeletons. Next, their pelvic bones would lance their hides. Their backs bowed, and they would begin stumbling with small, weak steps. Watching it broke a man's heart right along with his wallet.

"Dan'l, *this* child is a sinner," Snowshoe said thoughtfully, studying the herd at rest. "But you don't chaw nor hardly never cuss to speak of, nor never pick no fights. *Why* would the Lord test you like this?"

"Punishment," Dan'l replied, "for consorting with a sinner like you."

Snowshoe started to protest, but Dan'l waved him silent. "Ahh, I'm joshing you, you old fool. Mister, I've dog-eared my Bible, and I *still* don't know why the Lord keeps accounts like He does. It's His business, I reckon. Man proposes, but God disposes, and *there's* an end on it."

"Shoulda knowed you'd side with Him." Snowshoe sighed and added in a longing tone, "I still recollect that last meal your Becky cooked for us! Hot beef. And biscuits so light they needed holding down! Potatoes, gravy, greens, with huckleberry pie for dessert. Then a tall mug of ale and a good chaw. Gaw!"

"We got to git," Dan'l snapped, tired of being reminded of what he couldn't have. "Quit battin' your gums and go take up the drag."

Onward they pushed, Dan'l riding point, the Indians riding as swing men on the flanks, and Snowshoe bringing up the dusty rear. The Lord finally did take some pity on the weary men and horses: Good grass appeared over the next long rise, and soon the water was both more plentiful and more drinkable.

When, by Dan'l's rough estimate, they were within fifty miles of the Mississippi River, nearby twisters gave them a scare. But again the Lord watched over them. The dark, whirling funnel clouds bounced off to the northeast, sparing them.

"See?" Snowshoe demanded, "That 'ere's two pieces of good luck in one day! Mebbe we'll make it after all, by the Lord Harry!"

"Mebbe," Dan'l replied cheerfully. But nonetheless, his thoughtful, penetrating gaze was aimed toward the distant river, still well out of sight.

Even the Apache Grayeyes and the Papago twins were now in high spirits all the time, as were the newly fattened horses. All this alerted Dan'l. He had learned the hard way that the best time to expect trouble was when all seemed well.

Too, there was his last sighting of the Pacing White Mustang. Dan'l had been pondering that for days. Very little was wasted on him—not everything in life was an omen, but a smart man erred on the side of caution where signs were involved.

"Tell you what, hoss," Dan'l told Snowshoe. "Lansford Stratton ain't the kind of man to do anything by halves. After we bed down tonight, why'n't you boys hold the herd here a bit? Let this coon scout on ahead for a little look-see near the river."

Snowshoe scowled. "Now who's the calamity howler? Boy, we *kilt* them renegades! Could be a scout'll take two days exter, Boone! Goddamn ye, I need—"

"Tobacco, tea, whiskey, sugar, uh-huh, I know. Set it to music, nancy-man. You heard the plan."

"I heard a cat's tail! Dan'l, we're nigh home free! Why mark time at the finish line?"

But Snowshoe had been far too quick to assume their luck had changed for good. After twisters, torrential rain, choking dust storms, wolves, Spanish soldiers, flies, scarce graze, and poison water, it didn't seem likely that fate could have much left to dump on them.

But she did. And this final blow was the worst.

All throughout this drive, rattlesnakes had been

a constant nuisance. But luckily, they had not so far been encountered in large, concentrated numbers. That changed dramatically when Dan'l led the herd through a stretch of sand hills and rock outcroppings.

Later, when it was far too late, Dan'l cursed his own carelessness. He *knew*, damn good and well, that rattlesnakes liked to establish huge dens under outcroppings in sand. He also knew that late afternoon was a dangerous time, for snakes would be out in the sun. But his mind was too much occupied by Stratton.

Dan'l, out front on point, was first alerted to trouble by a screaming racket of frightened mustangs behind him. He drew rein and looked over his shoulder.

"Good God a-gorry!"

A calico filly had reared up almost vertically, frightened eyes all whites. And Dan'l's lips parted in revulsion at the sight of perhaps a dozen rattlesnakes hanging off the doomed beast!

A stallion on the right flank bolted, more snakes streaming from its legs and underside. Now Dan'l saw that one stretch of sandy ground was writhing with hundreds of enraged snakes.

What Dan'l had feared most happened next. Poco Loco bolted, and with the master stallion panicked, a headlong stampede was underway!

"Gentlemen, it's now been confirmed by two mirror signals from Sabine Lake. Boone is coming. And that resourceful bastard has indeed got himself a herd of scrubs."

127

Hugh Gilpin, newly arrived at Frenchman's Lick, finished his report from out West. He, Lansford Stratton, Lev Vogel, and "Nika" Bulgakov were inspecting the positions of Vogel's men near the river.

"Remember, Nika," Vogel reminded his lieutenant. "After tonight, no more squad fires. Just smudge pots to keep insects off. Cook over firepits deep in the trees, but only at night so there's no sign of smoke."

"Yes, the readiness is all against Boone," Stratton chimed in. "We cannot and must not assume that Boone will not scout ahead. But I agree he is unlikely to actually cross the river—unless, of course, we carelessly give him reason to."

"It's also critical," Vogel told Bulgakov, "that no one opens fire until hits are assured. Yet, wait too long, and they'll get ashore. Timing will be very important."

"Whatever happens," Gilpin warned, "do *not* be lulled into complacency. Mirror flashes also confirm that Boone has killed two of the best warriors in the Brasada country. You have my cast-iron guarantee: Boone is a serious threat."

Stratton nodded, savoring snuff in his upper lip. "Hugh's right. True, up in Yadkin County, the Boones have their own bench at the debtor's court. Nor does that untutored bumpkin possess the mentality to understand proper horse-breeding. But as a fighter the man is tenacious."

By now the group had paused near a buckboard used to haul oats for the horses. It was hidden in a thicket about thirty yards back from the river.

The Cherokee Princess Sarah Ferguson, Sha-hee-ka to her people, was securely lashed to one wheel of the buckboard.

"I want her gagged starting tomorrow morning," Stratton said. "No warnings to Boone."

Vogel cursed. In the sawing flames of a nearby fire, the damage to his face was clear. His nose was badly swollen, and a blue-black mouse had puffed one eye nearly shut.

"I say we execute her immediately for the murder of Armand," Vogel said. "Why save her? Your plan to let the men enjoy her is foolish. Take my word for it—by the time a man managed to subdue her, he would be too weary to enjoy her. Not to mention in too much pain. I say kill her!"

Stratton smiled his wire-tight, mirthless smile. It failed to include the corners of his mouth. "That's a poor idea, Lev. And a waste—in more ways than one. This little firebrand and Daniel Boone are former battle companions. You see, their criminal machinations almost cost me my fortune once before."

Hugh Gilpin nodded. He liked the strategy shaping up here. "Like her," he said, "Boone is foolishly loyal to a fellow campaigner. You're suggesting, milord, that just in case Boone proves even more resourceful than we expect, it might be good to have her on hand."

"Precisely," Stratton nodded. "A sort of assurance, if you will."

The woman's harsh bark of laughter startled all of them.

"You big *men*," Sha-hee-ka said with open con-

129

tempt. "Daniel Boone won't bargain with cowardly murderers like you. I warn you now, and this place hears my vow: You had *better* kill me, you white-livered poltroons! For I will surely kill you."

Stratton tried to stare her down. But in truth, the steely conviction in her dark eyes unnerved him, and he averted his gaze.

"On second thought," he told his companions, "gag that whore now."

It was not the initial stampeding of the herd that Dan'l feared. These were horses whose lead stallion had bolted; unlike cattle, they would not run as a group. With stampeding cattle, Dan'l knew he could throw them into a mill—turn them in a circle until they slowed down. But not with horses—they would soon break down the herd formation and scatter to hell and gone, never to be seen again.

Dan'l knew there was only one chance. Poco Loco had to be stopped without killing him. As much as Dan'l hated the chancy practice of "creasing"—grazing a horse's spinal nerve along the top of the neck with a bullet to temporarily stun it—he realized there was no other option.

"Snowshoe!"

Dodging panicked horses, Dan'l searched desperately for his friend. Nobody was better at the dangerous trick of creasing than Snowshoe Hendee.

But when Dan'l finally spotted him, his heart turned over. The old trapper's mule had slipped while turning on a patch of slick grass, and Snowshoe was down, wild horses plunging all around him. Even as Dan'l watched, however, the protective Malachi rose to his feet and quickly stood over the huddled form of his master, shielding him.

Snowshoe was safe, but useless to Dan'l for right now. Either Dan'l tried to shoot that lead stallion himself, and damn quick, or all was lost.

His opposition to creasing had kept Dan'l from ever trying it. But Snowshoe had mentioned something about aiming either for the withers or about one foot behind the ears. Dan'l swung his right leg up and hooked it around the saddle horn. He steadied his rifle muzzle on his thigh and brought the wooden stock up to his cheek.

This was a tricky business even for a man who was good at it. Most often, the bullet either missed completely or killed the horse. Dan'l aimed for the withers, prayed God's guidance for the bullet, and squeezed off a round.

A dust puff shot up behind the stallion's neck, and Poco Loco collapsed as if his bones had turned to jelly. Whether dead or stunned, Dan'l didn't know yet. But already the panicked horses were slowing—this was unknown range to them. They would rather cluster close to a downed leader than run freely in strange country.

Snowshoe crawled out from under his heroic mule, all in one piece.

"No eat this one, uh?" said an admiring Grayeyes. "Goddamn good *mula*!"

Snowshoe joined Dan'l as he rode forward to check on the ominously still Poco Loco. Their faces were brassy in the fading sunlight.

131

Dodge Tyler

"Quick thinkin', Dan'l," Snowshoe praised. "If he's dead, why then he's dead. You gave it your best shot."

"True nuff, hoss. But happens he *is* dead, you know the rest won't leave him. They'll stay right here, and they'll scatter when we try to drive 'em on."

"Ahuh. That's the way of it. Can't see no blood," Snowshoe added hopefully.

A moment later, even as the two men drew closer, the stallion's rear legs twitched. He lifted his head and neighed authoritatively to his herd.

Snowshoe, Dan'l, and all three Indians loosed a whoop.

"You done 'er, Boone!" Snowshoe yelled. "You goldang Kaintuck he-bear, you *done* 'er!"

"Get a rope over him," Dan'l said wearily. "And let's get this herd bedded down at least a mile past them snakes."

Dan'l gazed east, toward the Mississippi. "I got to get riding on that scout. I got me a God fear we're heading right smack into a hell-buster."

Chapter Fourteen

All through the night Dan'l rode hard to the east. By dawn, the grass was frosted and he was chilled clean through to bone. But the plucky Kaintuck was now only about a mile west of the ferry at Frenchman's Lick.

Pale mattresses of fog floated over the brushy hollows. Under a new sky like pewter, Dan'l searched out a deserted bear's den in the hills. He led the dun to a nearby pond fed by a quiet rill. Dan'l slipped the bit and loosed the cinch. There was no need to stake the dun—Dan'l just left a drag rope on him, knowing he would stay.

The weary explorer rigged a quick rabbit snare, then slept like a dead man until late afternoon. He woke up ravenous and found a skinny rabbit trapped in the snare. Dan'l dressed it out and roasted it on a spit. The meat was tough and greasy and needed salt, but it blunted his hunger.

By now the sun was setting in a burst of scarlet glory on the western horizon. Dan'l caught up his well-rested pony and headed for the river. He avoided the twin ruts of a wagon road, instead taking an old trail that was now grassed over. Dan'l paid special attention each time the dun raised its head up, ears pricked forward.

The crude settlement at Frenchman's Lick had quieted down for the night. The huge, three-raft ferry, now idle, was secured by heavy ropes to stanchions on the west bank of the river. Somewhere in the darkness, an old hound bayed mournfully at the moon.

Dan'l edged wide around the sagging livery barn with its water-stained boards. Across the way, the tavern door banged open, and a buttery shaft of light spilled out as two men emerged. Dan'l sensed the dun—overwhelmed by strange new smells—was about to whinny in nervousness. Quickly, he slid forward and pinched the horse's nostrils shut. The last thing Dan'l wanted now was to cause a ruckus and announce his presence.

There was very little good cover around here, Dan'l noted with forboding. He left his horse in the shadow of the barn and moved down to the water's edge on foot. Dan'l was silent and fully alert, moving with fluid caution like a tomcat on the prowl.

At river's edge, gnats were a constant swarm around his face. The cool night air was shrill with the chorus of "spring peepers"—Becky's name for those slippery little frogs that shone like slick ice even in moonlight.

But for a moment, Dan'l felt his throat tighten at the thought of Becky and the children back in the Kentucky River settlement. He immediately pushed these thoughts out of his mind. For a long time Dan'l just stood there studying the shadowy mass of the opposite bank.

The Big Muddy now reflected glassy sparkles in the moonlight. At first, Dan'l began to hope he was wrong about Stratton's plans. Dan'l felt reassured by the silence and stillness across the way. He could see or hear nothing that triggered an alarm.

Until, that is, he turned to his sense of smell.

At first, the odors, too, seemed routine and safe: the rich-silt smell of the river itself; the mustier smell of mudbanks and backwater bogs; the sweet, new-life smell of trees budding into leaf on the densely wooded east bank.

But then Dan'l whiffed something else—a cooking smell, he finally decided. True, he could spot no fires. But the wind definitely brought his well-trained nose a familiar cooking smell.

Corn meal. That was it. A common enough food, all right. But this smell was strong—*plenty* of it being cooked. Not just supper smells from an isolated cabin or two.

Dan'l had soldiered enough to immediately think of "ramrod bread"—corn meal wrapped around and cooked on a bayonet, a staple of late-eighteenth-century armies.

Frustrated by the discovery, Dan'l muttered an oath. He had hoped to return and give the others an "all clear" for the last leg of this travail. But now he had no choice—that smell was in his nose, not his mind, and it sure-god wasn't squirrels making it.

No man survived long on the frontier if he took to ignoring signs. That meant that, tired as he was, Dan'l had to cross that damned river tonight and see what he could find.

Borrowing Dick's ferry proved easier than rolling off a log. Dan'l only had to make friends with the old hound sleeping on it, which didn't take long.

Dan'l was a strong swimmer, but he wasn't up to full fettle lately. Nor could even a strong swimmer manage a straight line through this river's main current. He might eventually fetch up on the opposite bank, all right, but half-dead and maybe ten miles downstream. The ferry, despite its size, was dark, weathered wood that did not reflect light. Dan'l figured he could slip across the shadowy river, at least until he cleared the main current. Then he could swim ashore.

The ferry was a rope-and-pulley rig, very slow but also very easy to operate by tugging it hand-over-hand along its fixed ropes. Dan'l finally neared the opposite bank and waded ashore in chest-deep water, leaving the ferry about fifteen feet from shore so it wouldn't scrape and make noise.

Dan'l waded up onto the bank and nearly collided with an armed guard at a picket outpost!

Luckily for Dan'l, both men were caught by surprise, and the Kaintuck reacted quickest. Dan'l came here to spy, not draw blood, but it was past all debate now. His knife was out of his boot, and slicing into throat cartilage, before the sentry could shrug his musket off his shoulder.

But now Dan'l knew he had to scout quick and make tracks out of here. Cold sweat broke out on his temples as he threaded his way through the trees, stomach sinking at what he saw.

Granted, these men now dug in for an obvious ambush were jackleg soldiers—undisciplined and more criminal than military. But they were at least five or six strong for every man in Dan'l's group. Well-rested, well-fed, and well-armed. The horses Dan'l spotted were feeding from nosebags— that meant grain, and grained horses would be strong, especially if well rested.

If Dan'l wanted to get his horses across the river, it was here or nowhere. At least, he thanked the Lord, he was now forewarned. Forewarned was forearmed. . . .

When Dan'l had the layout fixed in a mind map, he started to retreat toward the river. Then he caught an odd image in the tail of his left eye: a supple, shapely, clay-colored female leg.

Dan'l moved forward through some hawthorn bushes, parted them carefully, then muttered in a whisper, "Well, I'm a Dutchman!"

Sarah Ferguson, not looking as pretty as he re-called her, was lashed tightly to the wheel of a buckboard. A filthy rag gagged her mouth; her thick, beautiful black hair was dirty and tangled, full of twigs and debris. And she had been badly used lately: Scratches and cuts and bruises mottled her face.

Dan'l could see no guard, though voices were clear from nearby. He slipped forward and touched her lightly on the shoulder, feeling the half-dozing Cherokee start violently awake.

"Easy, girl, it's Sheltowee."

Dan'l pulled the gag from her mouth.

"Dan'l!" she whispered urgently while he began slicing through her ropes. "I'm not surprised to see you. But I *am* glad. I prayed to the Day Maker, and He answered."

"I ain't surprised to see you where there's trouble, neither. But what the hell's your mix with this bunch?"

"You," she replied promptly. "Those are Lev Vogel's jackals out there. Now Stratton's hirelings. No doubt you know why they're here?"

"Well, ain't *you* some pumpkins," Dan'l said with deep admiration. Sha-hee-ka was tied with several strong ropes. Dan'l was still sawing through the last one, taking care not to cut the girl.

"I'll wager you gave 'em trouble," Dan'l added. "You're a reg'lar hellcat in a fight. How'd they nab you?"

Sha-hee-ka was about to reply when Dan'l saw her eyes widen with sudden fear. Even before she shouted a warning, Dan'l tucked and rolled.

He had left Patsy in her saddle boot across the river. Now he came up squatting on his ankles, his flintlock pistol at the ready even before he spied the danger: Lansford Stratton and Hugh Gilpin, both arriving to check on their Cherokee prisoner.

Stratton wore ivory dueling pistols, mainly for show. But he had no thought of drawing on Daniel Boone. He spun on his heel and bolted, shouting a warning to the others.

Gilpin, however, had led fusiliers in King George's Redcoat Army during the French and Indian War. His blunderbuss percussion pistol was in his fist in an eyeblink. He and Dan'l fired at the same moment.

The blunderbuss roared like a small cannon, so close the powder flash singed Dan'l's beard. The huge lead ball seared Dan'l's left temple like a hot wire of pain. It cracked harmlessly into the frame of the buckboard. Dan'l's ball, in contrast, punched hard into Gilpin's chest, spinning him halfway around and blowing a fist-sized exit wound.

But a worried Dan'l knew it was no time to recite their coups. He could hear Stratton and somebody with a thick Russian accent ordering the men to arms. Already men were punching their way through the bushes toward the buckboard.

"Hold still!" Dan'l rebuked the squirming Sha-hee-ka, hurriedly slicing that last rope. It snapped, and he pulled the stiff, weakened girl roughly to her feet.

But it was no use. She had been tied up too long, and her limbs refused to cooperate. Even as musket fire began cracking behind them, Dan'l slung the girl over his shoulder and lit out.

Dan'l fought down his desperation and forced himself to think clearly. Returning by the ferry was out of the question now. And for the time being, he and Sha-hee-ka had bigger fish to fry than getting across the river.

"Daniel, you *must* leave me!" Sha-hee-ka begged him. Bullets were cracking limbs all around them now. "Why should *both* of us die?"

"Both of us . . . *will* die," Dan'l replied between ragged breaths. "All in good time. But not tonight, pretty Princess."

"No, Dan'l! If—"

"Shush it, girl, and take my pistol. The top barrel is primed and charged. Shoot the first sonofabitch gives you a bead! We ain't just running—this here is a fighting retreat!"

Chapter Fifteen

"Granted, Daniel Boone is fast out of the gate," Lansford Stratton admitted bitterly. "So henceforth, *we* must be even faster. No more of this passive strategy. Instead of waiting for him to come to us, we're going to him."

Lev Vogel was about to object to this when he caught sight of his minion approaching from the river. "Nika! Any sign of them?"

Bulgakov, chest still heaving from the chase, shook his head. "Boone came over by the ferry, but he wasn't fool enough to go back that way. He killed Montreal Jon at the picket post by the ferry landing. We lost them about three hundred yards north of camp. The Indian she-bitch shot Roland Trapp. Gut wound. He'll be dead before sunrise."

Vogel cursed in Russian, a coarse, guttural

string of harsh oaths that made Stratton wince even though he didn't understand them.

"That's four men already killed between the two of them," Vogel raged. "And we haven't even engaged them in a fight! Stratton, you swore up and down this mission would be like seizing a bird's nest off the ground—your very words, damn you! You didn't mention that nest had *eagles* in it!"

But Stratton, too, was angry. So angry the others could whiff it coming off him.

"You've lost three tin-penny soldiers," Stratton shot back. "Common riffraff and venereal-tainted drunkards. No shortage of replacements for *their* kind. But I lost the best man I ever employed. Gilpin was worth a score of your bloody, stinking shirkers."

"They're all maggot fodder now, Gov'nor, and Gilpin will taste like all the rest to a maggot."

"True enough," Stratton agreed, calming down some. "And if *we* come to loggerheads, Lev, Boone has won. Don't you see? This is his excellent treachery. That bastard has fought in the woods too long, has turned into a—Christ, into some damned combination of lone-Indian warrior and frontier ranger. He rips away at his enemy in quick, bold strikes. A piece at a time, until you're only the skeleton of your former self."

Stratton drew himself up in the moonlight, his face all shrewd angles and planes in the silvery moonlight.

"So we are going to take a page from Boone's own book," Stratton added. "We're taking the attack to him, on our terms this time."

Vogel frowned. "That means fording the river and penetrating even deeper into New Spain. There was nothing about crossing the river when we struck terms."

"Are you daft, man? We've lost the element of surprise now. Boone has more friends than a dog has fleas. If we wait here to attack, Boone will make sure there are plenty of witnesses. Never forget, these criminal rabble out here feel no ties to London. And for common trash, they have strange notions about their 'rights.' We could face outraged vigilantes."

"So we go on the offensive instead?" Vogel mulled this and began to like the idea. "It *would* get us away from witnesses," he conceded. "And as for Boone—they say a fish always looks bigger underwater. Out on that open prairie, Boone's backwoods bushwhacking will be useless."

"My point precisely, Lev." By now Stratton had regained much of his former confidence. "Our horses are well-rested and strong. Good breeds, at that. Boone has nothing but wild scrubs that've just crossed a scorching desert. If he tries to run, in all that vastness, we'll chase him down like hounds to the fox!"

Punching branches out of his face, bent forward under Sha-hee-ka's clinging weight, Dan'l summoned his last reserves of strength as he fled up-river.

In those first desperate moments of escape, bullets had begun to dangerously thicken the air. Dan'l heard them rattling through the trees all around them, crackling like hail on a tin roof.

Then Sha-hee-ka took his pistol. He felt her squirm around to fire. Dan'l heard a man cry out, heard shouts of warning. After that, the chase noises abated as the pursuers lost heart.

"Dan'l, you rest now!" Sha-hee-ka ordered when they were perhaps two miles upstream. "I can walk from here."

"I figured you could by now," Dan'l replied between ragged breaths. He added a sly grin. "It was just sorter pleasant to carry you that close—though Becky would have my hide for saying that. You're a comely woman, Sarah Ferguson."

Sha-hee-ka blushed with pleasure. "If you were not married, Daniel Boone, I would show you how shameless a princess can be."

She glanced nervously around them and added, "However, I would not choose this spot for it. Have they given up the chase?"

"I think so," Dan'l said. "But I don't trust sound and directions near a river. You know how it is. We *think* we been running due north. But we been following the river. For ought we know, we've doubled back toward the enemy."

Sha-hee-ka nodded, understanding his point. No river ever ran truly straight. Even when you couldn't see it, they turned, even ran briefly backwards, so you sometimes couldn't even tell the nose of a boat from the stern.

"Wherever we are," Dan'l said, "we've got to ford, and quick. My horse and rifle are waiting near the livery at Frenchman's Lick—leastways, I hope they are. You got a horse?"

She shook her head. "I trailed Vogel's army by water. But my bateau is south of their camp."

"Useless to us. Well, happens we can get to that livery barn," Dan'l said, "mayhap we can get you a horse and rig. But time's pushing. We got to git, and quick."

It was Sha-hee-ka, perhaps twenty minutes later, who made the discovery. The two of them were beating the brush near the water, trying not to sink in backwaters and dead pools, looking for something, anything, that might float them.

"Daniel! Look here!"

Dan'l joined her and helped the Cherokee lift an Indian dugout canoe out into the moonlight. It had been buried upside down in a tangle of vines and blue columbine.

"Been long abandoned," Dan'l announced, studying some scaly weak spots in the moonlight—rough-textured places where termites and water seepage had weakened the hollowed-out log. "But the paddles're both here, and they'll hold. Thakee Lord! Beggars can't be choosers, Sha-hee-ka. We can bail with my good boot. C'mon."

However, the dugout was in far worse shape than a quick moonlight inspection could reveal. Water spouts sprang up almost immediately; Dan'l furiously paddled while Sha-hee-ka furiously bailed.

The two friends ended up swimming after all. But at least they had cleared the main current before the dugout scuttled.

Soaked to the skin, both of them suffered violent chills as they fled back downstream toward

Dick's Ferry. Dan'l found his dun still patiently waiting in the shadow of the livery barn. All was quiet at Frenchman's Lick.

Not so across the river, where the mercenaries were camped: Now huge fires roared, and Dan'l could hear shouted commands.

"Let's borrow you a horse and make tracks," Dan'l said, lifting the beam that secured the doors of the barn. "We'll bring it back with us and pay for the use. Ain't no time now to roust out the owner. We got to warn Snowshoe and the rest."

"Warn them of what?"

Dan'l nodded across the river. "They ain't gettin' ready for a fandango. They're mounting up. Stratton and Vogel are turning their sneaky little ambush into an all-out attack."

Chapter Sixteen

When he was still a tad back in southeastern Pennsylvania, Dan'l heard the men around him talk about the "cowardly" style of Indian warriors—their penchant for surprise attacks and sudden retreats. For harassing a foe to death rather than going for the "manly and direct" kill, as a British infantryman was trained to do.

But then, in young manhood, Dan'l had been sickened by the useless carnage he witnessed while serving as a teamster for General Braddock's ill-fated campaign against the French. Row after row of stoic soldiers shot down because they refused to "cower" behind cover.

Dan'l respected bravery, but not pointless sacrifice of God's children. Those were human souls being cut down, not just pop-up targets. The point for any true warrior, Dan'l decided, was to honorably survive the present battle so he could fight the next one that was always coming. So Dan'l, too, had begun to emulate the "cowardly" Indians—and thus, to perfect a style of warfare uniquely suited to the New World.

"As you can see plain," Dan'l told the group gathered around him on a rocky bluff, "the attack is coming to us. I figure they'll be on us in two hours—happens we stay here, that is. But we're gonna run in the open, *and* we're gonna whale the snot out of 'em."

"Katy Christ, Dan'l," Snowshoe cut in. "This child ain't a-scairt to get his life over. But face it, Dan boy. We got the high ground here."

"High ground," Dan'l replied cheerfully, "makes as good a graveyard as low ground."

"Better," Sha-hee-ka chimed in. "Sheds the water off your bones better."

Snowshoe squinted suspiciously at the Cherokee, not liking her habit of speaking up when men were talking about important matters. But he looked at Dan'l again.

"Boone, you want us to run in the *open*? They's only five of us."

"Six," Sha-hee-ka corrected him. "Assuming you count as a whole man."

Despite a weariness that lay heavy in his bones, Dan'l had to stifle a laugh as Snowshoe sputtered like an outraged preacher.

"Five *men*," the Taos trapper reiterated stubbornly. "And one pretty gal-boy what thinks she knows a war whoop when she hears it."

"You're like most men when they meet Sha-hee-ka," Dan'l told his friend. "You can't credit a woman that pretty with battle kills. Them ain't horse-tails on her sash, Snowshoe. Happens you spoke the Cherau tongue, you'd know her name means Beautiful Death Bringer."

"Scalpin' a man," Snowshoe said stubbornly, "ain't the same as killing him. The Digger Injuns send their young boys out to scalp the dead."

Dan'l saw a storm breaking here and cut into the battle.

"Let it go, both of you. What we got to recall is that Stratton's bunch has only got the numbers on us in men. But *we* got the numbers in horses. And it's horses will save us."

Below and to their east, dust boiled on the horizon as the attack drew nearer. Tattered parcels of cloud drifted across a late-morning sky of bottomless blue.

"Some men never learn," Dan'l went on, "and Lansford Stratton is one of 'em. But Stratton is only dangerous on account of what his money can do. Now, as for Lev Vogel—like Sha-hee-ka here will tell you, Vogel is about two hundred pounds of *hard*. The man's been tempered in them Russian winters, I reckon. Got the endurance of a doorknob and the morals of a Cossack. That bastard would steal dead flies from a blind spider.

"But he ain't just mean, he's tough—tough as any grizz! I seen him get drunk once in Natchez. The man rolled off a house and busted his arm in two places. Mister, my hand to God, he stood right back up, set his own busted arm with a canteen strap, then bought him another bottle and clumb right back up on the same roof, one-handed."

Sha-hee-ka nodded. "He is like the cockroach. You can step on him many, many times, but he won't crush."

"That Nika Bulgakov ain't no barber's clerk, neither," Dan'l said. "But they only know one way to fight. Listen, 'Shoe—how's them animals holding up?"

Dan'l nodded toward the holding pen down below on the flat. He hadn't had time yet to inspect the animals since he and Sha-hee-ka had returned.

Snowshoe tugged at one of his beard braids, scowling. "Turrible, *that's* how. Graze has been so puny, some of the colts has got the scours."

Snowshoe met dysentery. Dan'l nodded. That was bad, but not yet tragic.

"Scours will clear with better diet," Dan'l reminded him. "Happens we *do* get them critters across the river, you'll have money to throw at the birds, you old coot. Now quit battin' your gums and lissenup."

Dan'l again pointed toward the holding pen. "Each one of us picks five of the best horses for his battle string. That'll be thirty animals total. The rest we leave right here with our reg'lar mounts."

"Leave—? You chewin' peyote?" Snowshoe demanded. "Leave my Malachi and your best dun? Stratton's scum will just throat-slash 'em along with the mustangs!"

"They'd like to," Dan'l agreed. "But they won't.

On account they won't *get* this far. Not if my plan
works, anyhow. Make sure you string all your ponies on a sideline, not a leadline. We'll need to
make a few more rope halters real quick, we ain't
got enough. Then I want you all to ready your battle rigs."

By now Snowshoe was thoroughly baffled. Not
so the Indians, however. The moment Dan'l mentioned a sideline, all of them exchanged approving
glances. This Sheltowee, their glance said—
though his home range was far east, clearly he
knew which way the western winds set, too.

"Grayeyes!" Dan'l called out to the Apache.
"Quick, show wood-foot here how to bump-and-
gallop."

The bump-and-gallop was a desert Indian technique for outlasting a superior pursuit force in
wide-open country. It developed out of the Indian
custom of always having several horses on their
string.

Grayeyes caught up five ponies and necked
them a few feet apart with a sideline through their
rope-breaking halters.

While the others watched, the Apache goaded
all five mounts to a gallop. Snowshoe goggled
when the nimble Indian abruptly leaped onto the
back of the next horse to his left. One by one, at a
full gallop, Grayeyes rode each horse in turn.

"You can do that easy," Dan'l insisted, "on account of the mustang's smooth gallop. *Don't* try it
at a run or a lope! They bounce too much. It's
chancy, all right. But a man can run all damn day
long without resting his animals."

"All right, so we outrun 'em. They'll still come back here," Snowshoe insisted, "and kill our stock."

"Running ain't but half the plan, hoss," Dan'l explained. "There'll come a time when the enemy's horses will commence to blow and falter. That's when we pick one horse on our string and cut it loose. We close in for the quick attack, score a kill, return to our string for the next pony, and do it over and over until Stratton's bunch are feeding worms."

"Nothing to it," Sha-hee-ka said. She and Dan'l shared a discreet grin when Snowshoe swallowed a nervous lump in his throat.

"Why . . . sure, sure," Snowshoe muttered. "Just turn and attack, just like that. Nothin' too it, just pee doodles."

"All right!" Dan'l called out to the rest, "cut out your ponies and get 'em strung. Let's get thrashing!"

When his own battle string was ready, Dan'l quickly foraged through his saddlebags searching for loose lead balls. His fingers brushed a folded piece of foolscap paper someone had tucked there.

Dan'l unfolded it and recognized the childish scrawl of his son Nathan: *Bee it ever so bumble, there's no place like comb! Hurry home, Papa, we love you!*

For a moment the big man could only stand and smile, missing his family so bad that he ached for them. *This*, he reminded himself through blurry waves of weariness, is why a man keeps on keeping on.

Then Dan'l gazed east and saw the attackers were getting dangerously close. He swung up into leather and adjusted his heavy gunbelt.

"Mount up!" Dan'l shouted. "One bullet, one enemy! And the good Lord have mercy on us all!"

"Why, Stratton, you fool!" Vogel exclaimed. "You've galled his side with tight cinching! No wonder he's rebelling. *This* is how the 'equestrian expert' treats his favorite horse?"

"My God, man," Stratton shot back as he examined the nasty girth gall on his mount's flank. "It's a horse, not my mother."

"Out here, *my lord*, a man's horse is far more valuable than his damn mother! By neglecting yours, you've forced us to halt. Well, how is it?"

"I'll brush a little linseed oil on it," Stratton said. "Be good as new. It's nothing. It's just that I've never pushed him this fast or far before—I swear, Lev, that cinch is set where it's always set."

Stratton rode a big chestnut bay with a blazed face—a good animal that had been neglected and badly used. "Rode hard and put away wet," in Vogel's pungent phrase.

"In other words," Vogel said, his flinty eyes scouring the western horizon, "the great authority on horses has never really ridden one hard before. Just Sunday strolls."

But Vogel's mind was elsewhere. He swore out loud and added, "What is that goddamn Boone up to? The fool is riding right at us."

"Let him," Stratton snapped, daubing linseed oil onto the gall from a little clay pot he kept in his pannier. "Boone's been listening to too many folk tales about his immortality. He's swollen with conceit. Thinks he's Robin Hood, or better yet David taking on Goliath, with a Biblical guarantee of victory. That rube bastard! We'll snap his spine."

Vogel, however, appeared less sanguine as he mounted again. His men—twenty strong and well-armed—were riding in five sets of four behind him and Stratton.

"Better form a wedge for defense," Vogel decided. He raised his arms in a giant *V* to signal the command. Then he slid his flintlock musket from its boot and rested the butt on his thigh, muzzle up.

"I don't know what Boone has in mind," Vogel said. "It looks like simple suicide right now. But that 'rube' wasn't born in the woods to be scared by an owl. He's got a plan, and we'd best be ready for *anything*."

Chapter Seventeen

Dan'l felt a grin tugging at his lips when he saw the attack force form into a wedge.

"Don't matter if you boys make an *i* and dot it," Dan'l vowed to himself. The way he had it planned for this fight, the "front" would be everywhere, the "rear" nowhere.

Dan'l had selected five ponies that he had broken himself. Now he rode the best of them, a ginger mare, as his pivot mount—the one he chose to saddle and use to anchor the string. The Indians, even Sha-hee-ka, had chided him for selecting a mare. But Dan'l knew from experience that mares were not only as strong as stallions, but less temperamental and more manageable.

The other four ponies on his string galloped on his left, necked about three feet apart. Snowshoe,

Sha-hee-ka, Buffalo Runner, Coyote Man, then Grayeyes followed Dan'l's instructions, leading their battle strings in a staggered echelon to his right and left. Dan'l found an echelon was most flexible, allowing for quick adjustments on the run.

"Hi-ya!" Dan'l yipped like a Plains warrior counting coup as he leaped onto the back of his next mount. "Hii-ya, hiii-*ya!*"

Even unshod hooves made rapid-drumbeat sounds on this solid ground. Divots of rich prairie dirt flew up behind them like flitting bats. They charged ever closer to the enemy, and Dan'l saw some of Vogel's men bring their long guns up to the ready. He knew they would soon be able to shoot horses at this rapidly closing range.

But Dan'l had deliberately attacked with a good wind at their tail. He knew that Sha-hee-ka and the other Indians would thus get better range from their arrows. And he and Snowshoe had already doubled their main powder charges from one hundred to two hundred grains of black powder—so-called "buffalo loads." They would lose some target control, but gain in maximum effective range.

"Fire!" Dan'l roared out, and Patsy kicked hard into his shoulder socket. That extra charge packed a wallop that skewed Dan'l crooked on his horse.

A dust puff just right of Vogel's horse told Dan'l he had missed. So had Snowshoe. But both shots landed close enough, considering the range, to jangle some enemy nerves. And favoring wind gusts also helped sail a few arrows into the midst of the attackers. True, they'd lost much of their killing velocity by the time they'd flown four hundred yards. But several inflicted minor wounds to men and horses. Once again, the fact of even hitting at all, at that range, unstrung some enemy nerves.

Dan'l was satisfied, for now. This first volley wasn't intended to decimate the attack force— only to rile them so they'd be sure to come after the smaller force with renewed determination and blood in their eyes.

It had worked magnificently. Dan'l reined hard right, veering toward the wide-open grassland to the south. His force followed suit—and so did Stratton's.

Now the chase was on in dead earnest, pitting Stratton's big, grain-fed, winter-stalled quarter horses against the scrawny, grass-fed, weather-hardened mustangs. And at first, just as Stratton bragged, the race seemed to be going to the stronger pursuers. Even constantly spelling their mounts with the bump-and-gallop technique, Dan'l's group could not initially match the long stride of these fresh, long-legged, seventeen-hand horses.

By then some of the attackers had edged into long-gun range. Dan'l heard muskets popping behind him, saw dust pluming up only feet from his string. But Dan'l—who had endurance on his mind, not a quick victory—had anticipated this initial disadvantage to his force.

Suspecting this might come, he had fixed the location of an upcoming spot in his mind, during his recent scouting trip—a wide, deceptively safe expanse of "solid ground" that was in fact riddled with gopher holes.

Using hand signals, Dan'l led his team in a skirting maneuver to miss the dangerous ground. Just as he hoped, the evasive move wasn't spotted by Vogel. He and Stratton led their force charging, hell bent for leather, directly over the treacherous surface.

By now, the larger force was close enough that Dan'l heard the curses and shouts of alarm, the hideous whinnying of injured horses as the ground gave way. Dan'l watched one galloping mount plunge a leg straight into a two-foot hole, snapping its leg bone like dead wood and tossing the rider headlong.

Dan'l's gambit had paid off. Vogel, cursing like a bull-whacker on a muddy road, ordered his men to halt amidst a tumult of confused and screaming horses and human tumbleweeds.

But Dan'l was in no mood to claim victory. This was a stalling maneuver, that's all. One small battle won in a much bigger campaign. There was still mile after mile of open prairie ahead—when the tricks ran out, Dan'l realized, there'd be no place to hide.

"Three horses had to be shot," Nika Bulgakov reported to his superiors. "And one man broke a shoulder in the fall. We have available remounts for two of the men. So that's two more Boone has taken out of the fight."

"See it, Lev?" Stratton demanded, his shrill

voice climbing an octave. "*See* how Boone operates? He's like God in the universe—everywhere felt, but nowhere seen. First we had twenty-four men, then twenty, now eighteen. The bastard chips away and chips away, like erosion. Goddamn that insolent knave!"

Stratton, suddenly frustrated to the point of rage, threw a temper tantrum. He slammed his tricorn hat to the ground, cursed until he was sputtering, then turned on his horse. In a furious temper, he lashed the poor beast over and over with the reins.

Stratton's fit was over as abruptly as it had started. In the embarrassing silence that followed his outburst, no one knew where to look. Finally, Vogel gave the order to mount up. Already, his anger spent, Stratton was scheming again.

"It's all right, Lev," he said, stepping up into a stirrup. "Hugh Gilpin made an interesting point in his final report: Boone makes himself vulnerable by foolishly employing so many savages. Indians exhibit less loyalty than whores! After we kill Boone, we'll simply pay the savages in trinkets to slaughter his herd. Our work out here will be done."

"You mean *if*, not *after*," Vogel corrected him. "And don't ever forget the old saying, *if pigs had wings, they'd fly*. At the outset of this campaign, you swore it was enough to destroy Boone's herd. You only wanted to keep these mustangs west of the river to protect your investments."

"Precisely, and that's still my main interest. But both of us will regret it if we don't kill Boone now.

When will we have this opportunity again?"

"Would you talk about an 'opportunity' to go to Hell? I still advise you to lower your sights, Stratton. Never mind killing Boone. Be content if we can get to his herd."

"I'm disappointed in you, Lev. The best way to hit the mark is to aim *above* it. We can get Boone *and* his herd. It's still three to one. We've got three days' rations—let's run them into the ground! We'll turn this 'living legend' into a very dead joke."

"Here they come again!" Sha-hee-ka warned from the drag position. "And fast!"

Dan'l's battle group had halted briefly to check their rigging and reload weapons.

Snowshoe, busy adjusting his leadline, called over. "What's the plan, Dan'l?"

"Ride like the dickens," Dan'l replied as he tightened Patsy's breech plug. "Them that falls behind are gone beavers. So don't."

"Why—you call that a plan?"

Dan'l slapped his hat against his thigh, shaking off the top layer of dust. "It's better than a poke in the eye, I reckon. Gee up!" he shouted, pressuring the ginger into motion with a flex of his thighs.

"Orphans preferred!" Snowshoe bellowed out from behind him. "But say, bachelors will do! Come west and die with Dan'l Boone, Christians!"

Dan'l shook his head, gauging the distance between them and their pursuers. It narrowed even as he measured.

"You're a plumb good sort," he told Snowshoe,

"even if you do smell like a bear's cave. But you got a mouth on you, 'Shoe, and it's forever whining."

The two friends exchanged a few more familiar insults. But before too long, with the advantage clearly on the pursuing force's side, Dan'l and Snowshoe were locked in grim silence, fighting for their lives.

They fled back toward the direction of the endless sagebrush mesas called Wild Horse Desert. Each rider spent only a few minutes on any pony before "bumping" on to the next.

The plucky little mustangs, manes and tails streaming, were holding up well enough. But their scant diet lately was showing. Stratton's group steadily gained. Each time Dan'l chanced a glance back, they were a little closer.

Tarnal hell, he admonished himself. *Happens you called the wrong play, Boone, you've killed five good friends.*

That thought fired up Dan'l's determination. He took a sudden chance and slewed around quick on his tailbone, his balance on the horse precarious as he got off a quick snapshot. Dan'l felt a little surge of victory when a horse beside Stratton's suddenly stumbled, then fell, crushing its rider.

"Target!" Snowshoe bellowed. "That's Kentucky windage, Dan boy!"

But laugh on Friday, Dan'l thought, weep on Sunday—the very next moment, their celebration died a-borning. Vogel's flintlock puffed muzzle smoke, and Dan'l watched the back of Coyote Man's skull lift off like the lid of a jar.

Dodge Tyler

The dead Papago's brother cried out as if he, not Coyote Man, had been hit. Dan'l hated like hell to do it, but he had to threaten Buffalo Runner with his pistol when the grieving Papago tried to halt and retrieve his brother's body.

"Nobody halts!" Dan'l roared out. "They're closing in to easy plinking range. There's naught else for it: Keep your eyes on me and move when I do. On my command, we turn about face and *attack*!"

Chapter Eighteen

One moment, the force under Vogel and Stratton was leading an attack. Then Dan'l signaled to his companions, wheeled his string, and suddenly the attack force was under attack.

It was such an obviously foolish move that none of the mercenaries could even comprehend it at first. Dan'l saw that, and he knew it was critical to act fast, right *now*, with no thought about it! For in just a few heartbeats, the vital element of sur‑ prise would be lost.

Even as he wheeled round, Dan'l whacked at the leadline with his knife, cutting the ginger loose. The other four ponies peeled away to the north- west while Dan'l sailed straight into his enemy's teeth. His mocking, death-defying grin was back, unnerving all who saw it.

Nika Bulgakov suddenly loomed in front of Dan'l, a big man on a big horse, his face surprised but his reflexes those of a wild animal. He dropped the muzzle of his flintlock to the level, finger twitching the trigger even as Dan'l slumped hard right.

The Russian's lead slug whiffed past Dan'l's ear, like a hornet buzzing. Then Patsy jumped in Dan'l's grip, Bulgakov's face melted in a red smear, and Dan'l roared out "Kiss for ya!" even as he tossed Patsy into his left hand and opened fire with his pistol, emptying both barrels into enemy horses.

All this transpired in mere seconds. His firearms empty, Dan'l peeled hard right and caught up with his string. But the ginger was doing fine and had plenty of bottom left. Dan'l decided to stick with her.

Unfortunately, there was simply no time to recharge his firearms. His companions, too, had scored good hits, and now another five or six of Vogel's men were dead or out of the fight. But Coyote Man was sorely missed now, even though Grayeyes fought like three men.

The attacking force was on him again, swarming, less organized but still very deadly. Using his flintlock as a battle club, Dan'l knocked a man from the saddle in a vicious swing that dislocated the mercenary's jaw.

Dan'l's eyes sought Vogel and Stratton, but dust was swirling everywhere now, and it was impossible to make much sense out of the mounted melee. Then, for just a moment, the dust cleared, and an icy hand gripped Dan'l's heart—Snowshoe's horse had just been shot out from under him.

Snowshoe whumped hard to the ground and rolled, then lay dazed. An attacker with a saber leaned low to decapitate him as he flashed past. In a move inspired by pure desperation, Dan'l snatched the knife out of his boot, hurled it hard, and saw the blade slice into the mercenary's meaty thigh. It was not a lethal hit, but it threw the man's aim off—his blade parted Snowshoe's red hair, but drew no blood.

Still, Dan'l had only purchased a few seconds. Snowshoe was slowly struggling to his feet. But he had no horse, and another rider was bearing down on him.

Dan'l cursed, for he was at least twenty yards too far away to help in time. But suddenly, Sha-hee-ka streaked into the picture. She leaned dangerously low from her little claybank, seized Snowshoe by his big leather belt, and bodily dragged him out of harm's way. It was a struggle to keep his head clear of her pony's hooves.

Sha-hee-ka was successful only because Dan'l and Grayeyes assisted the rescue by riding in front of would-be attackers. But even as Sha-hee-ka dragged Snowshoe to temporary safety, Dan'l saw his and the Apache's fates sealed: The triumphant attackers closed in a tight circle around them, hemming them completely in! Dan'l had no loads ready, and both of the Apache's foxskin quivers were depleted of arrows.

Now Dan'l's eyes found Stratton's through the yellow-brown dust swirl. The arrogant Tory's face was suffused with the flush of victory.

Despite his desperate plight, Dan'l's chief emotion was not fear for his life, but disgust. Lansford Stratton had been bone-idle all of his life, profiting off of other men's risk and hard work. He and his silk-breeches ilk represented everything Dan'l despised—so-called "men" who defined their worth in land grants and titles and inherited privilege. Not, as Dan'l's breed had done, through muscle and sweat and character forged in the cauldron of adversity.

Adversity like *this*. Stratton was drawing one of his pistols when the first muttering thunder reached Dan'l's ears—the vibrating rumble of many pounding hooves, approaching from behind a low ridge to the west.

"Dan'l!" Snowshoe's gravel-pan voice roared out. "It's the Pacer!"

Dan'l saw him come gliding over the ridge, magnificent in that brutal southwest sun, a blaze of white so glorious it hurt your eyes. But it wasn't the sight of the Pacing White Mustang that dropped Dan'l's jaw and made Stratton's face drain gray—it was the rest of Dan'l's wild-horse herd, charging over that ridge and straight at the battle!

"Good God a-gorry!" Dan'l realized that the Pacer had not only "stolen" the mustangs back— but he'd brought along the mustangers' regular mounts, too. But it all happened too fast to allow much thought. Vogel's men were not quick enough in facing the charge; their shouts of terror and confusion rang in the air as the mustangs plowed into the battle groups.

Dan'l saw a frightened Stratton barely make his escape back toward the river. Vogel, however, had no such luck. He wheeled his horse around, but collided with one of his own fleeing men and went sailing from his horse. Dan'l saw the Russian, eyes two huge white disks of fear, try to leap back on his horse. But his foot missed the stirrup by inches, and—screaming as if being boiled alive—Vogel fell back to the ground just in time to be trampled repeatedly by frenzied mustangs.

Dan'l, who could stomach almost any sight except a child suffering, had to look away, his stomach pitching. The Pacer, Dan'l realized, had hung back on the ridge, his favor done. And in that moment, Dan'l understood: This was turnabout. That magnificent animal was paying Dan'l back for the day when Dan'l kept Snowshoe from "creasing" the Pacer!

A few battered survivors of Vogel's "army" managed to flee behind Stratton toward the wide Mississippi. But Vogel and Bulgakov lay in the dirt, carrion bait, and Hugh Gilpin was dead too. Dan'l knew the war with Stratton was over for now—over for a long time.

"I thankee, boy!" Dan'l roared out to the Pacer, lifting his hat in tribute. Snowshoe, too, now recovered, lifted his ratty flap hat and shook it in triumph and respect.

But the Pacer, his obligations to a friend fulfilled, was already tired of human beings again. He neighed once, rose almost vertically into the air, and then wheeled and was gone—so sudden and quick, Dan'l already wondered if he'd actually been there at all.

"There's your money, Dan'l," said Abbot Fontaine, counting the last pieces of Spanish silver into Dan'l's palm. "That's eighty-two mustangs at twenty dollars a head. One thousand six hundred and forty dollars."

The horse trader winked, and added, "And I'll make the same myself when *I* sell 'em."

"Boone," Snowshoe announced drunkenly, for he and Malachi had both been tippling since arriving in Frenchman's Lick the day before, "we are now rich sonsofbitches! This child is headin' to New Orleans and buying him a whorehouse."

"Watch your mouth, redbeard," Sha-hee-ka warned him.

Snowshoe whirled on her and was about to insult the Cherokee. Instead, he raised his jug in tribute to the gutsy war woman who had saved his bacon.

"You're not only tough," he told her sincerely, "but pretty as four aces. A man wouldn't go to . . . uhh, soiled doves iffen he had a reg'lar gal like you to home."

Sha-hee-ka caught Dan'l's eyes and held them as she replied, "No, I am sure he would not need or want to."

Then, winking at Dan'l, the pretty half-breed turned back to Snowshoe and said teasingly, "You know, Redbeard, if you did not *smell* so awful . . . who knows?"

Snowshoe was suddenly sober as a village alderman. He whistled to get the attention of a young boy passing by.

"Here, colt!" Snowshoe said, tossing the kid a two-bit piece. "Run git me a cake of lye soap."

Dan'l and Sha-hee-ka were still laughing when a roll of hoofbeats made everyone look upriver.

"Well, Gawd-damn!" Abbot exclaimed, pointing. "Snowshoe, your damned mule just stole one of my 'stangs!"

Dan'l saw Malachi fleeing along the bank. And running beside him was Poco Loco's favorite mare, the little blue with white stockings.

"That damned animule is so drunk," Snowshoe said, laughing, "he thinks he's a stallion!"

Dan'l counted twenty dollars in silver and handed it back to the horse trader. "That little blue stays with Malachi. He earned her."

Soon after, Snowshoe turned south toward New Orleans while Dan'l headed north for the Natchez Trace and the final leg home to his family up in Fayette County. Once again Dan'l Boone had blazed a trail where his critics said it couldn't be done.

And this time, he gave a fledgling nation a truly great gift: the finest horses on the North American continent.

DODGE TYLER

THE KAINTUCKS

The Natchez Trace is the trail of choice for frontiersmen heading north from New Orleans. But for Dan'l Boone and his small band of boatmen, the trail leads straight into danger. Lying in wait for the legendary guide is a band of French land pirates out for the payroll he is protecting. And with the cutthroats is a vicious war party of Chickasaw braves out for much more—Dan'l Boone's blood!

___4466-8 $3.99 US/$4.99 CAN

Dorchester Publishing Co., Inc.
P.O. Box 6640
Wayne, PA 19087-8640

Please add $1.75 for shipping and handling for the first book and $.50 for each book thereafter. NY, NYC, and PA residents, please add appropriate sales tax. No cash, stamps, or C.O.D.s. All orders shipped within 6 weeks via postal service book rate. Canadian orders require $2.00 extra postage and must be paid in U.S. dollars through a U.S. banking facility.

Name_____
Address_____
City_____State_____Zip_____
I have enclosed $_____ in payment for the checked book(s).
Payment <u>must</u> accompany all orders. ☐ Please send a free catalog.

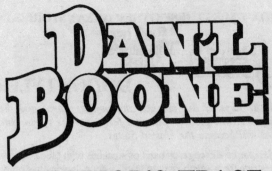

WARRIOR'S TRACE
Dodge Tyler

The Kentucky River has long been the lifeblood of American settlers near Dan'l Boone's home of Boonesborough. But suddenly it is running red with blood of another kind. The Shawnee and the Fox tribe have joined together in an unprecedented war to drive the white man out of their lands once and for all. And if Dan'l can't whip the desperate settlers into a mighty fighting force soon, he—and all of Boonesborough—might not survive the next attack.

___4421-8 $3.99 US/$4.99 CAN

Dorchester Publishing Co., Inc.
P.O. Box 6640
Wayne, PA 19087-8640

Please add $1.75 for shipping and handling for the first book and $.50 for each book thereafter. NY, NYC, and PA residents, please add appropriate sales tax. No cash, stamps, or C.O.D.s. All orders shipped within 6 weeks via postal service book rate. Canadian orders require $2.00 extra postage and must be paid in U.S. dollars through a U.S. banking facility.

Name_____
Address_____
City_____ State_____ Zip_____
I have enclosed $_____ in payment for the checked book(s).
Payment <u>must</u> accompany all orders. ❑ Please send a free catalog.
    CHECK OUT OUR WEBSITE! www.dorchesterpub.com

KIT CARSON

DOUG HAWKINS

The frontier adventures of a true American legend.

#1: The Colonel's Daughter. Christopher "Kit" Carson is a true American legend: He can shoot a man at twenty paces, trap and hunt better than the most skilled Indians, and follow any trail—even in the dead of night. His courage and strength as an Indian fighter have earned him respect throughout the West. But all of his skills are put to the test when he gets caught up in a manhunt no one wants him to make. The beautiful daughter of a Missouri colonel has been taken by a group of trappers heading for the mountains, and Kit is determined to find her—even if he has to risk his life to do it!

___4295-9 $3.99 US/$4.99 CAN

Dorchester Publishing Co., Inc.
P.O. Box 6640
Wayne, PA 19087-8640

Please add $1.75 for shipping and handling for the first book and $.50 for each book thereafter. NY, NYC, and PA residents, please add appropriate sales tax. No cash, stamps, or C.O.D.s. All orders shipped within 6 weeks via postal service book rate. Canadian orders require $2.00 extra postage and must be paid in U.S. dollars through a U.S. banking facility.

Name_____
Address_____
City_____State_____Zip_____
I have enclosed $_____ in payment for the checked book(s).
Payment <u>must</u> accompany all orders. ❑ Please send a free catalog.

KIT CARSON

COMANCHE RECKONING

DOUG HAWKINS

There is probably no better tracker in the West than the famous Kit Carson. With his legendary ability to read sign, it is said he can track a mouse over smooth rock. So Kit doesn't expect any trouble when he sets out on the trail of a common thief. But he hasn't counted on a fierce blizzard that seems determined to freeze his bones. Or on a band of furious Comanches led by an old enemy of Kit's—an enemy dead set on revenge.

___4453-6 $3.99 US/$4.99 CAN

Dorchester Publishing Co., Inc.
P.O. Box 6640
Wayne, PA 19087-8640

Please add $1.75 for shipping and handling for the first book and $.50 for each book thereafter. NY, NYC, and PA residents, please add appropriate sales tax. No cash, stamps, or C.O.D.s. All orders shipped within 6 weeks via postal service book rate. Canadian orders require $2.00 extra postage and must be paid in U.S. dollars through a U.S. banking facility.

Name_____
Address_____
City_____ State_____ Zip_____
I have enclosed $_____ in payment for the checked book(s).
Payment <u>must</u> accompany all orders. ❑ Please send a free catalog.